# BESS TRULY
## AND THE
# DESERT BRUJAS

BY JOE SLEDGE

North Carolina

*Gravity Well Books*

Publisher

For Callie

# Contents

Thursday, June 21, 1956
Three Winds, New Mexico

# CHAPTER 1

## A Cool Visit

Bess Truly listened to the incessant drone of her home's air conditioning unit running at full blast. She was laying on her bed, even though it was later in the morning. She was fully dressed, ready for the day in her new checkered shorts and shirt. Her cowgirl hat hung loosely on a bedpost.

But she couldn't find the motivation to get up. The house was cold inside, and the sun filtered through her window curtains at just the right light for her to sit inside and read. Her parents had been gone for a few days. Her mother, Portia Truly, was at the University of New Mexico meeting with other nuclear physicists for a week on a big discussion about using atomic power. Steve Truly, her father, a pilot, had flown down to the south to show off the Starlighter, an invention that Bess's mother and father had created.

The Starlighter was a new design of flying craft. It was a wide flat disc, powered by electricity, that made fast, hot sparks on the bottom of the ship, while an iridium ring spun around the outside to keep it balanced. It had a round set of fan blades around the cockpit in the middle that opened and closed to steer the Starlighter. It flew like a helicopter, but could move as fast as a jet plane. Steve had flown it to Holloman Air Force Base to show it off to the pilots down there.

Now Bess was alone. She was in charge of her ranch, the C Bar M, which had not only a large range for cattle, but also the only airstrip for miles and miles. She knew how to run the ranch well, even at fifteen. She had been working there for as long as she could remember. Her horse, Electra, was probably waiting for her right now to go for a morning ride. Electra would be getting restless if she didn't show up soon, Bess thought.

"At least it is something to do," she told herself.

She got up and made some noise, just to get the humming drone of the air conditioning out of her head. It was so cold, and constant, that it almost mesmerized her into sleep. "How did people get along without air conditioning?" she wondered aloud. Bess remembered the summer days when she was young, and just how hot it was in the long days of July. Before they had added the cold air to their big ranch, along with inside the bunk houses and cottages for the many ranch hands that worked for the Trulys. Her father had recently put in a pool  as well.

"But there's no one to swim with," Bess thought.

As she walked out of her room, down the stairs and out of her front door, she lamented that today, she was truly on her own. Her parents were gone, nothing special was happening on the ranch, and all her friends were doing other things. Her three best friends all had jobs or were busy. Jesse Armstrong, a year older than Bess at 16, worked days at his father's ice cream shop, and it was definitely busy right now. When he wasn't there, he worked on occasion at their radio station, playing the new Rock & Roll hits that she and and everyone at her high school in her home town of Three Winds liked.

Lydia Lanier took a summer job working at a local clothing store. She was the reason that most of the girls  Bess's age were wearing these cool shorts that Bess had on right now. The checkered patterns of black and white were all the rage in the big cities, but most people around Three Winds still wore blue jeans and thick shirts, even in the summer. They just stood around and suffered in the warmth. Lydia helped change fashion sense for the teens, and everyone else in town went with it. The shorts were more comfortable, and they looked great.

Bess's other friend, Aurora Baca, had gone north to visit with her extended family near Albuquerque, but would be back soon.

Bess wandered over to the stables, where big fans stirred the air, but blew dust and hay around in gauzy clouds. She needed to hose it down some, but that would wait. Electra snorted anxiously in her stall. "Okay, girl," Bess grinned at the horse, "we'll go have an adventure." She wasn't sure where, but anything would be better than the chilled boredom of hanging around the house.

Bess saddled Electra and rode her out of the stable. The heat of the day was in full swing. It was a beautiful, clear morning, with blue skies and not a cloud in sight. "Just when we could use a little rain and shade," Bess said to Electra. The horse neighed in agreement.

To their north, the town of Three Winds stretched across the flat prairie. It was a nice little town, with an ice cream parlor, a movie theater, two parks and a school.

Far to the south ran the river, now almost completely dry in the summer heat. Bess and her friends would swim and play there when the water ran, but it could be a dangerous place, as she had learned a few months ago during a flash flood. But there was no water in the river bed, the arroyo was all dried up, and as Bess looked back to the west, there was no rain on the horizon.

To the east stood the remains of an old, old mountain range. The rocky fingers of a curved ridge rose up, brown and hazy in the morning heat. Just past the ridge line was an open circle of a plain, that the locals called The Crater. Bess knew that there was a lot of work being done on the other side of the ridge. The U.S. Government had the land blocked off as big trucks, and bigger cranes, hauled out secret items from a terrible crash that had happened in the last month. Bess knew more about that than most. It was still hard to hide all that went on there, but the closed off roads and stern faced armed guards at closed gates kept most people away. The government was using a rail line belonging to the Trulys to load dark railroad cars with items from the site.

Bess had nowhere to go, really. She loped along the prairie, keeping an eye out for cattle, until she came to a fence line. Getting off Electra, she went over and shook the wire. It was taut, and the fence posts barely moved when she pulled. "Even the fences here are standing still, Electra," she said. Bess had no one else to talk to.

Even though she was in charge, Bess had little to do on the ranch. The hands were all run by their foremen, Joel and Manny. "We still need a relief foreman. Maybe I could hire someone myself." They had recently lost one of their foremen, and Bess stared at the far distant Crater as a reminder of just how that had happened.

But even hiring new workers wasn't what she should be doing. She had little choice left. The breeze picked up, a hot wind that didn't cool her down any. "Let's get back home, girl. There's nothing to see out here." Bess noticed even the bugs were staying in the shade. They didn't want to be out in the sun, either.

Bess turned Electra to head back home. The ranch was a distant line on the horizon, but not a far distance for her horse. "We'll go back for some cold water and a treat, girl," Bess rubbed Electra's neck. "or maybe a Popsicle." She fanned herself with her hat, then plopped it back on her head. With a soft tap to Electra's haunches, and a gentle cluck, Bess and Electra headed home at a confidently quick trot.

Bess looked up over the the blue sky, still blue on blue, rich with color and not a blemish on it. Bess wasn't sure what she liked better, looking up at a clear New Mexico sky, or looking down from it. Bess was already an experienced pilot, and could fly most light planes. She had flown the Starlighter on multiple occasions. "I'm probably the fastest fifteen year old in the world," she thought.

It took several minutes, but she finally made it back to the ranch. Close to her house, she again heard the constant humming of the air conditioning units with their fans spinning, and electrics singing to make the cold air. It was the same constant droning sound that put her to sleep at night, or bored her this morning.

The sound was so common to her that it almost drowned out another sound, very similar. Only as it got louder and Bess got closer to the stables did she realize that the sound didn't come from her home, but above it.

Bess put Electra back in her stall, but her head was looking up. She almost absentmindedly ran a hose of cold water into Electra's trough. As she turned off the hose, she heard a plane buzz over the ranch. It was planning to land, she knew, because there was no where else around for small planes to touch down.

Bess threw a carrot to Electra. "I'll come back in a bit, girl. Let me see who this is."

It wasn't anyone local. Several people had bought small planes since her father Steve had built the airstrip, but none had flown out this morning. It had to be someone coming in from somewhere else. And no one had made plans to stop for services, for gas, or to put the plane on the tarmac or hangars. This was an unplanned stop, she was sure.

When she looked up to see what plane it was, she had a mixed feeling of concern and excitement. She recognized the plane as it flew over.

The plane was a Beechcraft Bonanza. She recognized it immediately because of the V-shaped tail. It was the preferred aircraft for rich doctors and businessmen.

"And G-Men," government types.

Bess not only recognized the type of plane, but who it was inside, even though she couldn't see that far up into the cockpit.

Bess started walking over to the airstrip as the plane descended onto the landing strip. It touched down with only the softest kiss, then slowed quickly. This was an experienced pilot, one who meant business. He didn't bother to glide to the far end of the runway, but punched the brakes and turned quickly onto the tarmac to stop the plane.

By the time Bess had gotten to the airstrip, the pilot was already out. It might have been the same pilot she had seen before with the plane. He wore a crisp Air Force uniform, dark sunglasses, and had a perfect golden blonde part to his short hair. The pilot stood in front of the plane, looking like he was waiting for applause.

He wasn't the important person in the plane, though. Bess knew that.

From the passenger seat, a man in a black suit and tie, crisp white shirt, and sharp cuffs stepped out. He was young, with blonde hair almost white, a California boy all grown up.

The Voice.

Even this was not who Bess thought was going to get out of the plane. It might not be as important as she thought.

The Voice was Agent Phillips, the G-Man, the man in the black suit, and one half of a team of federal agents that had been to Three Winds less than a month before. His other half, Agent Marsh, The Chair, the other nickname that Bess called them only in her head, was not in the plane.

"Surprising," thought Bess. "They usually travel in pairs."

Agent Phillips saw Bess coming over almost immediately. He began to walk toward to her, through a group of the local ranch hands who tended the airstrip. A couple of them began moving toward her, but Bess waved at them. "It's alright, I know this guy," she said confidently. With the bosses both gone, Bess was the boss, and the ranch crew was always going to make sure the boss was okay.

"What's your story, Agent P?" Bess tried to sound casual, but when these guys showed up, something was happening. They didn't make social calls. "Where's Agent M?"

Agent Phillips tried not to cringe at the nicknames, including the "Agent". It was no secret they worked for the government, especially in their black suits, but he didn't need it advertised.

"Hey, Bess," Agent Phillips answered her. He smiled, but it was half hearted, and she knew it. "It's just me, Agent Marsh is busy. It's part of what we wanted to see you about."

"So, what's up?"

"It's about your father. He was down in White Sands, you know."

"Yeaaaaahh…" it was more of a question than a response by Bess.

"Well, we discovered some, curious things that may have been happening down at the Brokeoff Mountains, near the border. Agent Marsh asked Major Truly," Agent Phillips used Steve's former rank, as it was more comfortable for him to refer to Bess's father by a military term, especially when he is discussing a volunteer mission for the US government. "It wasn't far away, and we just wanted some pictures. He had plenty of range…"

"Did something happen to my father?" Bess asked.

"We don't know.

"Bess, right now, your father is missing."

# CHAPTER 2

## The Trust Of A Stranger

Agent Phillips spent about a half hour explaining what they knew about Steve Truly's disappearance. "We know he was okay. He landed somewhere near the border with Texas, and he said he had power then. He had plenty of food and water, and there are sources for water there, as well. He told us he was safe when he touched down, so we know he didn't crash, you don't have to worry about that.

"We just didn't hear back from him afterwards."

"Are you going to look for him?" Bess asked.

"That's part of the problem," Agent Phillips scratched his head. "First, it's in an area around the border, and we don't want to get too much attention. This isn't what we would call a military thing, and we want to keep it that way. And then, there's what he told us the last time we talked with him. He said, 'Bess will know what to do.' Does that mean anything? Why would he ask for you to do something?"

"So you can't go looking for him?" Bess asked.
"Oh, we are," Agent Phillips said, "But it really seemed like your father wanted you to be there."

"What was he doing there?" Bess was still puzzled and mad. Agent Phillips seemed to be purposefully vague. "What was he looking for?"

Agent Phillips looked around, as the ranch hands, still milling around not far from Bess, especially with what looked like a heated discussion, were possibly within earshot, too. He didn't say anything, but looked up at the sky.

Bess followed his gaze. Even though it was approaching noon, the clear blue sky held not only a bright sun, but a waxing moon as well.

She looked back down, leveled into Agent Phillips's eyes, just above his dark sunglasses that tipped down his nose. He said nothing, but raised his eyebrows in a wordless comment.

Two hours later Bess was in the front passenger seat of a pickup truck, towing her horse trailer, with Electra secured within it.

She had rounded up Manny, their relief foreman, to load the truck and drive her down past Roswell and Carlsbad, toward the Brokeoff Mountains. Manny had sat quietly through much of the trip. He was still new to the ranch, and had always been nervous and uncomfortable around Bess.

She thought he was just unsure how to act around her. He was comfortable on a horse, and ran the ranch really well. Bess trusted him implicitly, but he just was more comfortable around the rest of the crew than around teenagers, it seemed to her. Two hours into the three hour ride, he finally turned off the radio blaring in the truck to cover over the roar of the wind and tires. "I really don't think this is wise, Miss Truly," he absolutely refused to call her Bess. "I don't think your parents would like me sending you off into the wilderness alone. I really think we should wait until your mother gets back."
Bess had tried to reassure Manny, "My father asked me to come." It wasn't entirely true, but it was close enough for Manny.

He had at least insisted that a family member, a distant aunt, come up and stay with Bess for the night at a local motel, before starting off in the morning. They found their way into Carlsbad at a clean and cool motel, where they met his Tía Yesenia. Manny took Electra over to a nearby stable that would be more comfortable than stuck in the trailer all night while trucks roared by on the highway.

It had been a long drive for the both of them. Bess was worried about her father, and Manny was stressed over taking his boss, the bosses' daughter, out into the desert and turning her loose on a horse. By the time they had arrived, both were hot and hungry, Yesenia insisted on them going out to eat. Bess brightened at the idea. "A good meal will definitely help," she agreed. The next few days of being out in the mountains existing on dried food and canned vegetables while looking for her father wasn't going to be as fun as camping by the arroyo with Aurora and Lydia, where they could always ride back home in an hour.

Bess unfolded a map at the restaurant to show Yesenia where she was going. She couldn't tell Yesenia much, and Bess's Spanish was still not fluent. "I know he has landed there," she pointed out a spot close to the border. "And that he landed safely, so he had to find some flat land. And he said there was water, so it has to be near a running river or stream. I'm going to put in at this trailhead and go west, climb these residual mountains, and see if I can see him." Among the gear she packed away was a pair of powerful binoculars.

Yesenia squinted at the map in the soft light of the restaurant. She could see well, but Bess could tell she was more worried about where Bess was going. "You can get there, *sí*, there is water there. And animals, too. Elk live there in the winter. Not much now, fox, rabbits, you won't find animals to hunt easily. They will be scared. Are you going to hunt for food?"

"No," Bess insisted, "I'm not taking a rifle. I'll pack in some dried beef, and enough food for five days. I don't plan to be gone more than two."

"Are you sure you don't want a rifle?" Manny worried.

Bess insisted she would be fine. "I'll have my Zap-Gun."

Bess always carried her Zap-Gun with her. It was her mother's invention. It was a tool for working around the ranch. Her mother, Portia Truly, had invented the Static Discharge Device, a tool that gave off different levels of an electric beam. At low power, it worked like a flashlight, brightening the way in the dark or sending signals. At higher powers, it could weld fence wire, dig a hole, or blast through a hill to make an opening. Bess had learned quickly just how powerful and useful the device was. She and her friends Aurora and Lydia all had one when they rode together. While her mother didn't like the term, her father had jokingly called the tool a Zap-Gun, and nicknamed them the Zap-Gun Rangers. The name stuck, and all of them were proud to be in the very exclusive club.

It would be a useful tool, and a good deterrent, but not really used for hunting deer. Bess wouldn't have time to do any of that, anyway. She wanted to find her father, and get back to civilization as quickly as possible.

Yesenia seemed worried more about something else. "Do you know these lands?" she asked, almost quiet and suspicious.

"No, not really, but I've been out in the prairie all my life. This is an easy trip for Electra and me. Don't worry."

"It's not that," she became even more conspiratorial. "There are stories about this land. The mountains, they are home to many mysteries."

Bess was intrigued, but she tried not to smile. There were always local legends, old tales of ghosts and monsters that lived in distant and inaccessible lands, just far enough off that no one could go check on them easily.

But why would Yesenia try to scare her off?

"You won't believe me, but the locals here, and to the south, they know. It is said to be a place where people fly without wings."

Now Bess was intrigued, for real. Anything that was about flying, she was interested in, and this could have something to do with her father.

"Do you mean like updrafts?" she made a motion with her hands, lifting up off a cliff, "like the wind blowing up a mountain?"

"No, not like that," insisted Yesenia. "People have seen them, from far away, but recently, within the past week." Then she leaned across the table.

"The..."

She was interrupted by the food being brought, and stopped short, as if she didn't want to say the magic word and have the story interrupted. Bess could barely look at her plate, as she waited for the server to leave and Yesenia to go on. "Go ahead, say it." After her last month, Bess wasn't about to doubt anything out of hand.

"The *bruja*. The witches, they live there, and fly across the mountain tops. People have seen them, from far away. They are dark shapes that fly from mountain to mountain."

Bess had heard the tales and legends of the bruja, the strange people who could walk in the clouds, or fly on broomsticks from mountain point to mountain point. She doubted they were real, probably just a mix of things blowing in the wind, and legend meant to scare little kids into coming in at night.

"You will see the *bruja* there," Yesenia insisted, right in front of a forkful of food. She took a bite, chewed, swallowed, and deftly continued. "They will see you first. But you will see them. They will not come near you, they do not want to be discovered, but they can be seen."

Bess took the story in stride, listening intently as Manny's tia told her story. Bess just hoped it didn't scare him enough to insist on taking her back to Thee Winds.

But instead, the three of them went back to the motel, where Yesenia was quiet and respectful of Bess getting ready for her journey.

"Sometimes we all must make a trip. It is a passage of responsibility, and we have to be trusted to do the right thing. I spent much of my youth trying to be adventurous, to learn, to be responsible, and many people tried to stop me.

"But they all failed."

Yesenia took Bess's hand, as any kind aunt would do. "I can see you are both prepared and willing for this adventure, and I want to give you my trust, the trust of a stranger, that I know you can do this."

And with that, Yesenia turned away and let Bess get ready for bed. She needed a good night's sleep after all she had been through today, and for the long journey tomorrow morning. She had to get up early, earlier than usual.

Bess went to sleep with the soft glow of a neon sign filtering through brown curtains in her room. She slept heavy and fitfully, dreaming of witches on broomsticks, chasing her on Electra as she tried to shoo them out of the air with her Zap-Gun.

# CHAPTER 3

## Blazing A Trail

Morning came early, very early, for Bess. She had
Manny drive her to a trailhead as far as the truck
could go without bouncing Electra around in her
trailer. The sun was barely coming up and the air was
deliciously cool. It was going to heat up quickly, she
knew, and she wanted to make good time while the
sun still had to rise. Electra snorted happily with the
scent of new smells in the air, and new places to go.
Bess felt the same excitement.

Bess had consulted a topographical map of the
area, as well as plotting with her compass, and
comparing the directions and landmarks on the paper
map with what she saw. She then looked at a silk
handkerchief she had bought the evening before,
where she had traced the outlines of the land onto the
white material. Additionally, she had written the last
known location of her father, marked it with an x,
and plotted a basic distance to the spot. Bess had

asked Yesenia to write something in Spanish on the cloth as well. Just in case something happened out there, she had gotten Manny's tia to write "Estoy perdido o herido. Por favor ayúdenme con comida, agua y medicinas. Llévame al pueblo más cercano para que pueda contactar a mi familia. Serás enormemente recompensado." Bess could speak Spanish well from learning it from her mother, and she even understood some of the local Apache and Navajo. But if something happened to her, if she was injured, someone could find this and understand to take her to help. It was something she learned from her father when he was a pilot during World War II.

But Bess wasn't worried about that now. The land of southern New Mexico, and close to the south, Texas, stretched out before her. The distant mountains looked old and jagged, dry, brown, until they reached to high heights, where pine trees somehow grew in the cooler, thinner air. Morning clouds rose up on the sides, whipped by the wind. They looked like the fingers of ghosts, reaching over the spires of the mountaintops. The plains opened below her. They were familiar, but at the same time, different to Bess. The prairie around Three Winds was robust, ever changing. It had trees and brush that grew in fits around the land that was a crusty sunkissed yellow. Here the flat land was almost smooth, but covered with a small brown and green brush called Chihuahuan scrub. It grew there as well as to the south, in the desert of Mexico where it got its name.

To Bess, it just meant that there was life there, something she always appreciated. She had seen some of her prairie die, and didn't want to see that ever happen again. Even here, at the edge of a dry desert and mountain chain, she saw the life that flourished in the land. She knew that was a good sign, and a good omen. She would find water, shelter, and soon enough, her father.

She rode along her own trail by setting a course toward a landmark far in the distance that she knew was about west southwest. It would lead her to a canyon that cut through the lower mountains, and to a river bed. After that, she would follow it as far as she could, until she came upon a low set of hills that she and Electra would have to cross.

That was the tough part. She didn't know what she would find there. Getting up the hills would be difficult, but she knew Electra could handle it. The question was whether or not there was a way down.

"At least it will let me get a look on the other side of the land," Bess said to her horse and to the soft wind that blew about her. There was no one else around that could listen.

She rode along at a soft trot. Electra could go for hours like this, and Bess only had to hold the reins to show her horse that she wasn't falling asleep. It was like Electra knew the direction she was supposed to go instinctively. The far off point on the mountainside was kept right in front of Electra's nose while Bess simply sat in the saddle.

Bess would occasionally lift up in her stirrups, just to look around. It also took a little pressure off of Electra's back and Bess's hips. "I think you can handle this ride longer than I can, girl," Bess quipped.

Electra neighed in agreement.

The long ride ended after two hours, when horse and rider found their way through the pass and into a wide riverbed, where a continual wash of fresh water rolled over polished white sand and stone. Bess stopped to let Electra drink her fill, while Bess drank from her canteen. "This looks like as good a place as any for a morning snack," she said as she dismounted. Electra drank greedily, then snacked on some of the sweet brush that grew up around the river bank.

Bess took the time to look at her map. It was still early in the day, thanks to her pre-sunrise start. She had made good time so far, but the rest was going to be slow going. "No rest for the wicked," she said, listening to the soft echoes of the canyon in front of her. "And no slowing down for us, Electra. Let's get going." She hoped to make it to the next landmark by lunch, where she could take the saddle off her horse and let Electra relax a bit.

Bess climbed back onto Electra, and began the slow trot down the stream.

"At least it's a little cooler here by the water, isn't it, girl?" Bess tried to keep up a conversation with her horse, partly to avoid the loneliness of the trip, and to keep Electra engaged. There were few things worse than a bored horse, Bess knew.

Bess wasn't bored on the ride, though. The view was beautiful. It was rugged, green and rocky, with steep cliffs that jutted off at sharp angles and hidden holes that probably sheltered snakes and birds during the heat of the day. In the winter, the river would be full of elk, drinking to their satisfaction. In the spring, she bet this river didn't run like the shallow creek it was now, but a deep and flowing pool of cold water, melted off the tall mountains from winter frosts.

After another three hours, Bess finally made it to her next landmark. She hoped she was there, at least. It looked like the right place, another notch in the mountain walls. This one led to a small plateau that looked out toward the west and south. The huge wall of the Brokeoff Mountains were now to her back, with the narrow canyon that she had followed behind her.

The river sprawled out into an arroyo of shallow water, only a few inches deep. Tall trees stretched both skyward and outward along the river and flatlands. They took hold where ever they could, which created a tangle of roots that looked like a knot tied by ancient giants, then just left to weather in the summer heat. Oak and maple grew tall, but along the banks grew wild honey mesquite trees, which offered the shade Bess and Electra needed more than anything.

"Lunch time for me and you," Bess said. She climbed off of Electra and took off her saddle. With the trickling water and green grass, it was unlikely that her horse would run off, but Bess didn't want Electra to get spooked, so she tied her to a lariat and pin, which gave Electra plenty of room to graze and prance, finally free of her burden.

Bess sat under the tree and ate a peanut butter sandwich. There wouldn't be much time for peanut butter sandwiches in the next few days, she knew. She had a small loaf of bread, and a good choice of canned and dried food, but she wanted to find her dad and get back to civilization as soon as possible.

"What were you doing here, Dad?" she said only to the map. "There's nothing out here. This is only a good place to come if you are going on a long ride. Or you want to hide." Bess pondered that last thought. Her father wasn't trying to hide. He was sent out here, to look for something. Agent Phillips had said nothing, because he didn't want to be heard. But he had looked up at the moon.

About a month before, Bess had done something that she wasn't really supposed to talk about. She felt like she shouldn't even think it, even out here. Strange occurrences had happened around her town, and she had discovered it was an invasion by the last survivors of a strange colony from outer space, a group of military men from the moon, who tried to take over the Earth. But they had been stopped before they had a chance. She had been there, and had been part of it. "A big part," she had to admit to herself.

"But we stopped them," she said, "we stopped them all."

"Didn't we?"

The day stretched out ahead of her, and her curiosity and concern won out over the summer heat. She needed to know where her father was, and he was probably on the other side of that plateau. She rose up, waved her hat onto her face, took a long swig of water from her canteen, and called to Electra. "Time to saddle up, girl. We gotta go to work."

It was harder work, finding a path up the plateau. The map she had showed the topography like the rise of the mountains around her, but no one had been out here to map trails, much less cut any. "That's why they call us trailblazers, huh Electra." Her horse snorted a sarcastic agreement. "I can always count on you to agree with me."

Finally, after a long walk with lots of turns and cutbacks, and a few dead ends, Bess found a path that walked her up to the plateau and the view beyond her. It was a gorgeous landscape. The trees were big and green, with dark, dark wood, and bigger mountains to the east of her than she had seen before. She stared out into the Guadalupe Mountains. "We must be in Texas now," Bess said. She half laughed at her next thought. "Maybe my dad was just trying to go home for a bit." Her father was originally from Texas. He had moved to New Mexico partly to start his ranch and airport, but mostly because he had married her mother, who was from there.

"Now, where are you?" Bess said from the saddle.

She reached into a small pouch and pulled out her binoculars. She had no idea what she was looking for. Maybe a glint of shining iridium from the Starlighter. Smoke from a campfire. Hopefully not a clearing with wreckage. But Bess kept remembering what Agent Phillips had told her. Her father had landed and said he was safe. It was only after that they lost contact. So if she found the Starlighter, she should find her father.

She scoured the vista with her binoculars. They got her closer to the far off area where her father should be, but she saw very little. She would just have to get closer.

One last look, and Bess noticed something. She saw vultures, or turkey buzzards, flying the thermals over the rolling mountains, swirling like smoke caught in an updraft. That was nothing new. They usually did that. It wasn't a sign of anything dead on the ground. If there was, they wouldn't be in the air, she knew.

Then, out of the corner of her view, she saw another black shape fly across the sky. This was no vulture. It moved fast, and straight. Bess was startled by it, and tried to follow with her binoculars, but it disappeared. She pulled them down and looked with her eyes.

Far off, near a series of cliffs and low rugged hills, she saw it, a strange black shape, about the size of a person, as it flew through the air, then fell, disappearing into the treeline.

Bess felt her body go cold.

"The *Bruja*..."

# CHAPTER 4

## Safe In The Dark

"If Mom could see me now."

Bess had been spooked by the *bruja*. She had no one around her to pretend to. She was scared by the sight of a figure flying through the sky without wings.

"Without a broom," she told herself. "If it was a *bruja*." There was no way it was a flying witch. It couldn't be. She had watched for another ten minutes to see if it reappeared. "Well, maybe only thirty seconds," she admitted to her own mind. Time was working a little differently right now.

Right now time seemed to be ticking fast for very little progress. Yes, she was scared, but she was worried, too. There was something out there, right where her father was supposed to be, but there was no sight of him, and there was something flying through the air, and into the trees. It wasn't a crow or a vulture, Bess knew that. She could still see the buzzards, circling endlessly, far less perturbed than

Bess was. She tried to convince herself that it must be something normal because it didn't bother the birds. But that little part of her mind that worried, the voice in her head that told her to do something, it was shouting down any ideas to the contrary.

So now she was struggling to find a way down the other side of the plateau. She had gotten off Electra and led her by the reins on a narrow and slippery dry path. It was just too steep to risk riding her horse. Some spots were nothing but gravel falls that Electra skipped and slid sideways, always surefooted, but still uncomfortable.

Bess was less comfortable, and certainly less surefooted. She was no mountain goat, she told herself. Twice she tumbled in the loose gravel, ending up on her back. "I'm glad I didn't wear shorts today," she commented about her fashion choice of thick denim. Her jeans had kept her legs from being torn to ribbons by the sharp stones underfoot.

But that was what she was thinking of when she had said "If Mom could see me now." Bess wasn't one to rush headlong into trouble. She wouldn't do something headstrong or risky. But if there was a problem, if there was someone in danger, she never shirked her responsibility. She would plunge forward when anyone else might turn back. So when she saw that strange thing flying through the air, it only took moments for her to start riding down the hillside toward the unknown. Her mother had always pointed out that Bess was usually the first person to run to help someone.

It wasn't like she could just rush headon into danger. Bess found her way down the hillside, after a long forty five minute struggle just to safely, sort of safely, make her way toward the bottom of the slope. She wasn't even in the flat part of the valley yet. Bess had to stop and collect her wits. She also needed a new compass direction. She was a little turned around after all that sliding and going sideways to keep from tumbling down the cliffs.

Bess took out her map, and tried to figure out where she was. "I'm definitely close to Texas, or in it. And that's got to be on the Texas side." She looked at the higher peaks of the Guadalupe Mountains. The landmarks were harder to determine now that she was lower, and had to look through trees. She wasn't about to go back up the hillside, not with all that loose rock. "We may have to find another way out of here, girl," she admitted to Electra. When she found her father, and if the Starlighter was working, Bess realized that there was no way to get a horse in the tiny cockpit. She was riding out on horseback no matter what. Another glance at the map and she saw a few small towns far to the east and south, within a long day or two ride, but nothing she couldn't do.

She just had to find her father first.

She sighted on a tall spire, one that seemed to be just east of where she wanted to be. If she rode that way, when she got to the base of the next mountain range, she should be able to turn south, or southwest, and follow the treeline, where there hopefully will be water and shelter.

And ultimately her father.

She realized about four hours later the other problem she had with time was how it was running out. Daylight was long, but the day wasn't. Electra was tired, and needed rest every three hours. She could be ridden all day, as long as she got breaks, with the saddle off, and time to move and scratch herself, to rub against a bush or graze on some sweet grass in the forest. The sun was still up, but beginning to set. Bess knew she would have to stop for the night.

She found a decent place, with a small stream, and an open area for Electra to be left. Bess gathered some fallen branches and cleaned a spot for a fire. Witch or no witch, she would need some light for the night. She twisted and broke some twigs, and found a few larger fallen branches, which she piled up. Bess drew her Zap-Gun, dialed it up only to a lower power setting, and sent out a blue spark to the wood. It popped and snapped, with a few pieces flying out in orange embers. Then the fire blazed forth. No need to bang rocks together, or rub sticks, Bess joked. She had all of one small tin pot in her pack, which was exactly the number she needed. Some water from the stream, and a bag of dried beans went in, which was going to be good enough for dinner for the night. She tore off some of her bread to soak up the flavorful water at the bottom of the pan.

The fire crackled to a low flame after Bess was done with dinner. She pulled out her Zap-Gun and a small device her mother had made for times like this. It was a tiny Sterling engine, a simple device that turned a wheel when one side of the engine was hotter than the other. She placed it on a rock, the bottom facing the heat of the fire. The little motor began spinning in a soft *clickityclick*. Attached to it was a tiny electric motor, which spun making power and sending it to the battery pack of her Zap-Gun. She had barely used it, and had a spare power pack, but it was always a good idea to keep it charged.

Then with her belly full, she unrolled a bedroll and tucked her bag under her head, with an extra t-shirt draped over it as a pillowcase. Electra snorted, then rolled into her own grassy bed.

"So, I'm a softy," Bess answered Electra's comment. "Go to sleep."

Bess fell into a deep sleep as the embers of the fire crackled softly at her feet. She dreamed of black shapes coming out of the dark to chase her and her father into the tall trees of the forest.

## CHAPTER 5

### Footsteps To The Sky

Bess awoke with a start. She was in a strange place, and uncomfortable from sleeping on the ground. Then she remembered where she was, and looked around to see her campsite in daylight.

Electra stood in the nearby field, already awake. She had slept like she usually did, standing up, which let the horse be immediately alert for threats out in the wild. "Better than a guard dog," Bess called out to Electra, who snorted happily at the compliment.

The fire had gone out, so Bess quickly restarted it with a few branches and a snap from her Zap-Gun. It was still early, and Bess was happy to get up and going, but she needed to take care of herself and Electra. She would do no good if she was hungry and her horse was tired. She put on her little tin pot with a lid over the fire. She would heat up some oatmeal and sugar with some water for her. While the water boiled, Bess first tossed some carrots she brought for

Electra. Fresh vegetables wouldn't last long out in the heat, so it was best if Electra ate them now.

Bess was never a big fan of coffee, but now she saw why the old cowboy movies always had them drinking it by the gallons. She could use something to perk her up.

With breakfast quickly done, Bess put out the fire with water and dirt. She stirred the ashes and poured more water until the pit was cold and smelled like an old fireplace. The cinders were wet and looked like a horrid porridge. But it was definitely out.

She saddled Electra, put her foot in the stirrup, and lifted herself up by the saddle horn. Almost immediately, her morning aches went away. To some, riding for a long time was painful and uncomfortable. To Bess, she felt like she was back home in the saddle. She consulted her map, and then dotted where she thought she was on her handkerchief as well. The paper map was already getting a little worn on the folds.

She looked up, through the trees and to the far south, to find the same jutting point she sighted on yesterday. It would be tougher going, through the wooded part of the wilderness, because she could change direction without knowing it. She would have to consult her compass often, and couldn't move as quickly, just when she thought she was finally getting close.

At least the ride was enjoyable. The trees were thick with green leaves, and the ground soft from years and years of untouched leaf litter. The temperature, already cool in the early morning, was about ten degrees milder than out in the unshaded prairie. Bess wished she had time to explore more thoroughly, but she stayed at her task.

She sited often down her compass, always trying to stay on the same path and direction. She noticed twice that she had drifted to the west, and did her best to correct her path, but every step out of a straight line was time wasted. She needed to find her father, or find out where he had been. He may have walked out on his own, she worried, and she would only be chasing his ghost.

Bess had that thought on her mind, which helped her push out the thoughts about the *bruja* that she had seen. "I have to stop calling it that," she had told herself, "until I know what it really was." There was no way it was some flying witch, living out in the Guadalupe Mountains, no matter what Manny's tia had said.

"Nothing is going to sneak up on you, is it," Bess patted Electra. When Bess kept her eyes ahead, on the lookout for the next place she would go, Electra could see all around her, even behind. The woods were full of life, with birds and antelope squirrels flitting around the trees. Even with all the movement and new sights and scents, Electra kept to her regular forward trot. If anything bigger than a javelina tried to get close to them, Electra would alert Bess immediately.

Bess chose to take a long morning break, get Electra's saddle off, and rest, so that she could take a shorter stop around lunchtime, and hopefully move on into the low ridges and mountains ahead. It took a long, long time. Bess was getting impatient.

By noon she had reached the foothills of the mountain chain that ran through Texas and into Mexico. It was a wild mix of residual boulders that dotted the land along with tall trees and twisted mesquite. It was the change from forest to mountainside. Along the west facing cliff were jagged outcroppings, tall spires, tree covered mountaintops, and shadowy caves. She knew there must be hundreds of them. Carlsbad Caverns in New Mexico, near where she had spent last night, were famous caves in nearby mountains. The caverns had been "discovered" about sixty years earlier, by a cowboy named Jim White, who explored and promoted them for years. Bess knew they were just one of many, and the caves could hold secrets that may never be discovered.

One of them could also hold her father, waiting out rescue in the cool shade.

But where was the Starlighter?

She finally got to where she guessed it would be on the map. This was where Agent Phillips said her father had last planned to go. It was an open flat land. It wasn't the best place to land, but more like the only place. The area was clear of trees and rocks, flat, and firm. It was almost perfect for landing and taking off. The only issue might be the thousands of pebbles that would ping off the Starlighter's ignition chamber.

The Starlighter flew by electricity, much like the way Bess's Zap-Gun worked. It was a disc, but the bottom was a shiny polished point, where a spark was ignited, and the heat popped off at a very high temperature and a bright light. The hot air would push out the sides of the base, lifting the Starlighter into the air. It took a lot of energy, and the Starlighter would lift up with a rapid *thumpthumpthump* that Bess always referred to as its heartbeat. It needed a clear, clean spot so that the rocks didn't get caught up in the fans that helped direct the Starlighter in which way to go. Also, any scars or scratches to the base would make the Starlighter work less efficiently. "Maybe that's what happened to him," Bess thought. "The Starlighter got damaged and couldn't take off well." But what would he do next? He still would have called for help, or would have alerted someone with the radio.

Worse than that, when Bess finally got to the clearing, it was empty, empty, empty.

Bess rode Electra in a slow, wide circle around the field. "This is the perfect place," she said. "If I had to land anywhere around here, I would land here. It's the best place to land for miles.

"So why isn't it here?"

Bess got off Electra and walked the ground, looking for clues, maybe a message, or signs of humanity. But there wasn't even a footprint. "It's all smooth, not even a rock, like it's been blown..." she realized why it looked like a perfect landing spot. Looking at the edge of the field, where trees and scrub brush surrounded it in almost a perfect circle, she saw bits of debris, rocks and twigs, all embedded in the trunks of trees and leaves of the bushes.

"He *did* land here," Bess exclaimed. "But then he took off again. Where would he go?"

Bess found a small patch of grass with some shade and staked Electra so she could graze. Then she looked up at the tall mountainside above her. It was covered with ledges, craggy overhangs, and numerous tufted brush, all green and dark.

Bess began to climb. If she could just get clear of the treeline, just a little bit, she could look out over the forest below and see if there were any signs of the Starlighter.

She set her sights on a large open outcropping. It was probably big enough to land the Starlighter there, maybe bigger than the field below. But she would see the Starlighter easily in the day. The silver craft should be glinting light like a diamond in the summer sun right now. But there was nothing up there but rock and dull brush.

When she got to the top of the ledge, it was even bigger than she thought. "It must be fifty yards wide," she noted. Far below, she saw Electra contentedly grooming the sweet wild grasses that grew nearby. To the south, she could even see a small pool of water from a stream that must have run straight out of the mountain.

Then she noticed something. She had seen it when she had climbed up the ledge, but it didn't register with her at first. The big mesquite brush grew all over the mountain, including at the side of the ledge she was on. But this set of bushes were drying, like they were dead, or recently cut. Bess walked over and touched it. The leaves came off in her hand.

The brush was loose, as well as dead. Someone had cut the mesquite and placed it there in a huge pile, over fifty feet across. Bess grabbed one big branch and pulled. It gave way easily. As she threw it aside, she noticed how the branches made marks in the sandy ledge. All around where she stood, the ledge had been swept, but not like the field below. It was uneven, with big strange circles, about six feet wide, overlaying each other. It almost looked like the beds spawning fish made in the water. But this was the dry desert.

Then she noticed the footprints, too.

Someone had stood there. More than one. Now Bess took in more and more, in between the big circles. It was if they all stood there, and tried to sweep their tracks away.

"But none of them lead away from here," Bess noticed. "It's like they just...." she looked up into the sky, "jumped."

# CHAPTER 6

## Old Enemies

Bess looked from her feet, to the footprints, to the sky, and then, "Do the *bruja* live in this cave?" That was nonsense. There was no such thing as a flying witch, she told herself for the umpteenth time. She didn't know why she needed convincing. But she was going to look behind these cut brushes. *Bruja* or no *bruja*, someone had been there, and they might know what happened to her father.

When she looked past the big brush camouflage, she saw it hid a giant cave entrance. The ledge worked as a shade, making it incredibly dark from even only a few feet in. The opening was large, almost as large as the landing she had stood on. It was wide and taller than her. But it was dark as pitch. Bess felt very, very alone.

She pulled her Zap-Gun, dialed it down, and squeezed the trigger.

From the thick glass rings on the barrel, a blue light glowed brightly, lighting her way as she pointed it down to see where her steps would take her. There was no way she was going to risk stepping into the darkness of an open crevasse and tumble down into a sheer cave. Bess carefully took one step in front of another.

Comfortable now that the cave was only at a slight angle, she stopped and shone her light along the walls. They rose up much higher than the mouth did. "It's bigger on the inside," Bess said. Her words echoed into the darkness, carrying on and on into the depths. "Well," she thought, this time silently, "the *bruja* know I'm here now."

If the cave was wide, it could hold anything, she realized. Bess turned the dial up on her Zap-Gun, just one power level higher. It made a much brighter light, and a tiny spark crackled at the bare point of the tool.

The bright blue light lit up the cave like a lantern.

Bess was stunned at what she saw, sitting there, in the middle of the cave.

"He must have flown it in here with the landing pads up," she said, with a tone of congratulatory awe. She looked at the way the blue light glistened and gleamed. Any person who was enamoured of chrome clad cars would be envious of the bright shine this had.

In front of her, still, quiet, and perfect, in the dark, stood her father's ship, the Starlighter.

"I can't believe he got it in here!" she half whispered. She was afraid if she said it too loud, the magic would end and the Starlighter would disappear like a mirage.

"Dad?!" she shook the reverie from her head. She had come here to find her father. He had to be near. Bess ran toward the Starlighter, looking in the cockpit. "Dad!" she called again, louder this time.

But no shadow stirred from above, through the open parted fans, inside the glass dome cockpit.

Bess got up to the middle of the craft and shone her light around in a feverish search. "He has to be here!" she cried. She had come this far. She climbed up to look in the window, thinking maybe he was asleep, or worse, hurt and trapped in the pilot's seat. But the cockpit was dark and empty, with not a sign of power.

Bess hopped down, and began to look around.

"Okay, don't panic," she told herself. "Think it through. He put it here. No one else could do that. He had to put it here. But why? He had been sent here to find something about the moon, about what happened last month. He's not here, but he will have to come back."

Bess looked around, wondering what else was in the cave.

Then she saw something in the back, farther away from the entrance. It was hidden in shadow, and dark, not shiny metal like the Starlighter, But it was big.

Bess started walking toward it. As she got closer, the shape became more defined. It was round, but thicker, and dark green, like it was absorbing the light.

Then she recognized it. And she felt her blood go very cold.

Bess fell to her knees, the strength gone out of her legs. She felt her grip loosen on her Zap-Gun, with her finger coming off the trigger.

And then the cave went very dark.

## CHAPTER 7

## High Noon

Bess had recognized what she saw immediately, even though she had never seen it before. She had seen things like it, though, and the memories flooded back to her.

She picked up her Zap-Gun, fighting the temptation to turn it up to full power and just start blazing. A flick on of the light, and she began to shine the blue illumination over what she had seen.

It was a flying saucer. She knew it. She knew it because she had seen several, up close. She could tell from the rounded, blunt edges, the hard lines of the vents and propulsion system on the bottom. The three legs that extended down were on industrial sized circular hinges that allowed the gear to fold up into the fuselage. This one was vaguely triangular, not circular like the ones she had seen before. It had a large bulbous cockpit over the top that was rounded off like a spine down the middle of the craft. The front had two large glass portholes, huge and bulbous, sticking out of what must be the cockpit. It looked a lot like a giant deranged insect.

Underneath, Bess saw a long closed section of doors. "That's where it keeps its stinger," she said.

Bess knew exactly what this was. It was a strange space craft from the moon. She knew it because just a month ago, several of them landed in the Crater just outside of Three Winds. A group of men from the moon had invaded, hoping to stage a sneak attack from a hidden base in an open area, where they could take over the military bases and then control the air with a devastating ray gun weapon. Bess had discovered them when they had shot her down on the first flight of the Starlighter. With a lot of help, Bess and her friends had defeated one of their smaller flying saucers, and then the Army came in and was able to stop the moon men, just before they could stage an invasion with a giant space craft. Bess and her mother had done their parts in helping to destroy the big ship.

The moon men had been captured and taken away. Bess thought they were good and rid of them forever.

But here sat one of their ships.

It was cold and dead, with not a light gleaming from it. The last time Bess had seen one of these it had pulsed with green energy as the ships extended their deadly ray guns from the hull and shot at her and Electra. The ships had devastating firepower, but took time and energy to recycle and reload. She had worn herself and Electra to frazzles trying to tear one apart and bring it down with her Zap-Gun in the sands outside Three Winds.

"But what was it doing here? And what does Dad have to do with this?"

Neither ship seemed damaged. When the Starlighter had been hit with one of those ray beams, it had shorted out half the electronics and bent the smooth iridium ring that orbited around the outside edge and kept the Starlighter stable. It had taken weeks to fix, and about all the iridium available in the entire state, the metal was so rare.

But this time, the Starlighter was fine. And the space ship behind the Starlighter seemed undamaged. It looked old, and was a little dusty, but it wasn't dented.

Then Bess realized something. The space ship was *behind* the Starlighter. It had to have been there first. And somehow, the Starlighter got parked in next. Bess admired the job done. "He had to fly it in here with the landing pegs up. It's the only way it would fit." She realized that only her father could have done that. No one else could fly the Starlighter that well, not even her.

"Which means he's alive." Bess convinced herself of something she wanted to be assured of. Her father had hidden the Starlighter here, and left it hidden. He may have found the moon men's space ship here and wanted to hide so that he wasn't discovered. It opened up so many questions in her head, but it always lead back to one big answer. Her father was alive. That was the important thing.

Now, how to find him.

Bess wasn't going to look around the dark cave for clues. She had already found what she was looking for. She knew her father wasn't there. He had to have gone somewhere outside, so she put her Zap-Gun in its holster and began to slowly back out of the cave.

The entrance was filtered by the leaves and branches of all the mesquite trees her father had cut to disguise the opening. The sunlight flitted through like gossamer over the dying leaves. She couldn't see out onto the landing, but the light was bright outside.

Suddenly, one of the shadows moved. Something, or someone, was outside the cave.

Bess had to hesitate to run. It could be her father, but then, it could be someone else.

Then she saw another shadow. It moved up on the ground, through the leaves. The shadows came up from her feet, which meant the person, now persons, making them, had to be coming down.

From the sky.

"The *bruja*..."

Bess had to see who it was. She wasn't going to get trapped in a cave, and she had to know if these people, witches, moon men, it didn't matter, had a hand in her father's disappearance. She stepped forward and shoved a huge branch of mesquite out of her way.

There in the clearing, on the big rocky landing, stood two figures. They wore the dark jumpsuits of the moon men, but other than that, Bess could make out no features. They both wore full face helmets, with dark lenses for eyes, and a strange grate or filter over their mouths. On their backs were small backpacks, with wide circular tubes or nozzles of metal, a dull silver or tin.

All of a sudden, Bess heard a hissing *whoosh*! From out of the clear sky, ten more figures fell, only to kick up dust just feet from before crashing to earth, where they landed with a soft bounce. All wore the same outfits, and all had the same...

"Jetpacks," Bess described them. "Or something like that."

It was out of the realm of a comic book, or Sunday matinee at the theater, but here they were, moon men come flying in to confront her. The same ones that came on that insect ship in the cave. And they had to know where her father was.

The twelve men just stood there, looking through those black lenses on their helmets. If they were trying to frighten Bess, it was working, a little. But she wanted to know where her father was, and they were going to tell her.

If they wanted a fight, they just found the losing end. Twelve of them versus one angry daughter. Bess drew her Zap-Gun and stared them down. "I've done this before," she said loudly. "and I'm the one still standin'"

Bess waved her Zap-Gun menacingly.

Then, ten more moon men fell from the sky.

And then, one more, landing only ten feet in front of her.

This one wore a leather coat, and stood a little taller than the others. And definitely closer. The leader, Bess assumed.

"You'll be the first one to give me the answers. Now, where's my father?"

She leveled the Zap-Gun at the chest of the leader, her eyes narrowing at him.

Then, he took his helmet off.

# CHAPTER 8

## The Bruja Flyers

"Easy now with that six-shooter, pardner," came a soft Texas drawl.

Bess had seen the moon men up close, and didn't like it. They were pale, white skinned, thin, with black eyes, and all sick from radiation. This was definitely not a moon man.

His hair was golden blonde and curled, a little messy and matted from being under the helmet. And he had tanned skin under a scruffy beard that hadn't been shaved in a few days. Bess recognized him immediately.

"Dad!" she screamed as she holstered her Zap-Gun. She ran to him, hugging him around the neck awkwardly. She felt the warm metal pack he wore, and the straps that held it tight to him.

"But, what are you doing with these moon men?" She was suddenly wary, her hand reaching again for her Zap-Gun in its holster. She may yet have business to do.

"Don't worry, kiddo," Steve Truly smiled his disarming smile, the one that told everyone that things were going to be okay. Bess knew that sometimes, he used that even when things weren't. But she took her hand slowly away from her Zap-Gun.

Steve turned around and said, "It's alright, this is my daughter, Bess."

With that, the group of about twenty two people began to remove their helmets. They all looked different without the shields on. Most still shaded their eyes, while a few pulled out dark goggles or sunglasses with side shades on them. They were still sensitive to light, Bess saw.

She saw something else, too.

They were women. And girls and boys. A couple were older men, balding or gray haired. None of them looked like the evil moon goons she had fought and defeated at the heart of her hometown. No black circles around their eyes, no heavy sweats or pale skin. They looked, well, they looked like... "humans," Bess realized.

The moon men had been human, but they were as inhuman, inhumane, as could be. Full of hate and greed, lust for power, only thinking of themselves. These people definitely didn't have that look. Bess stared at them, from one to another. They looked, Bess tried to ascertain what she saw.

"Scared?"

"Worried?"

She didn't quite figure out what it was, but then she recognized the look. It was the same one she had when she found out her father was missing.

"They aren't with those moon goons," her father used the term they had coined when the invaders had first been discovered in Three Winds. "They were trapped there. Remember the military telling us that there were some people who didn't want to come to fight? Well, these are those people." Steve went on to explain how they were refugees, escaping from deep within the last homes of the moon, built well underground, near the moon's south pole. They realized that no one was coming back after they discovered what happened to the first group. So they repaired one of the last ships they had, the insect like bus, and flew toward the only known location, one near where the first group had gone, and hopefully a place they would not be detected when they landed. They hoped to come ask for help, quietly.

"But they weren't really the last ones on the moon," Steve explained. "There were a few of those malevolent leaders left, with some willing soldiers, all waiting to be called down when the invasion succeeded. When it failed, they tried to enslave these people," Steve swept his arm around to take in the small group standing by him. "And their families. There's more of them, Bess, children, the elderly, all hidden around here."

"Why are they hiding?"

"Because that wasn't the very last ship they took. There's one more. They tried to take it out of commission when the escaped the moon, but they failed. The last remains of that totalitarian army that invaded us is going to come looking for their people, to take them back.

"But there's nothing left there. The entire place is either crumbling or radiated. They can't go back, but the bad guys want them anyway. They would rather force them, old people, children, babies, families, to go back and die on the moon, than come here."

"So what are we going to do with them here? Can we..." Bess looked around, looking for a physical answer in the wilderness. "just, walk them out of here?"

"That's only part of the problem," Steve shook his head, showing that it wasn't so simple. "Yes, we could do something like that, but, see, the bad guys, well, they may be coming for them."

Bess felt her eyes widen. The moon men were on the warpath.

"We need to find a way to hide them," Steve explained. "When they were first approaching Earth, they got a call, a demand, from the last people on the moon base. They were ordered to return or the people on the moon would come after them, take them, take their children, back. We think they were able to track the flying saucer to here. That's why we hid it, and hid the Starlighter. We don't want anyone seeing where they are. The flying saucer had some sort of tracking device, like the others did, the transponders like on our planes." Transponders sent out a simple signal of what plane was what, helping to identify and track them. "The pilots of the flying saucer were able to turn off the transponder once they discovered it. But their location, at least this general area, was already known. But the people left on the moon were coming after them. There was that thing, the bus," Steve pointed into the cave, "and one like the ships we saw, that could carry troops. The bus could carry more, so they took that. There were only two people who knew how to fly, a couple of old guys like me," he half chuckled, putting a lopsided grin on his face, making things a little less dire, "and they were both needed to fly that big old thing."

"So you flew it in there? And the Starlighter? To hide them? How did you manage to fly in through that narrow opening?"

"Very carefully," Steve laughed. Any time something was tense and needed precision, that was his advice on how to do it, "very carefully."

"What I had to do was charge their engines. They were all out. We had to drain most of the battery from the Starlighter just to get the bus to lift off. There wasn't much left after that, and you know how much power she uses to lift off. I had one shot for both. But I got the keys to fit." Steve seemed rather proud of himself.

Bess decided he should be. "That's some fancy flyin', Tex!" she dropped into her father's soft Texas drawl. "But how do we get them out?"

"That's the problem."

Bess looked into her pack at the Sterling engine. It would take, weeks? Bess imagined, to charge the Starlighter.

"I know what you're thinking, and I've already done it," Steve pointed into the cave.

The two walked into the darkness, and Bess lit her Zap-Gun. "See, look, your mother thought it would be a good idea to have a small generator, hooked to a windmill, or anything that could turn, as part of the Starlighter, for, well, *not* for something just like this, because who could have predicted that we would be stuck in a cave with a space ship from the moon?" Steve exclaimed.

Bess interjected with, "It's happened to me twice, now. I know that's not a lot, but it's about two more times than you think it would be."

Steve patted Bess on the shoulder and laughed. "That's why I need you here, cowgirl, you've got all the experience!"

He continued by pointing out a wire that ran from the Starlighter into the darkened depths. "There's an underground stream, not much, but it moves pretty fast. I stuck an impeller in there, I bent the blades on that little fan your mother made, and it's spinning in the water, making power. It's charging both crafts now."

He led Bess deeper into the cavern. It got cool real quick, and felt great compared to the summer sun of the day. She heard the water running down the walls. Shining her light, she saw the fresh water, from a spring or groundwater seeping in from above. It was cold and clean. Bess tasted it, chilling her as she licked the mineral water off her hand. "This will take forever," she said. "Why not charge the Starlighter first? And go for help?"

"That is part of the plan, but I didn't want to leave them alone, especially if someone came for them while I was gone. No, what I need you to do is ride back and contact Agent Marsh, tell him where we are, and he can figure out a way to send help. Right now, both ships are just getting to the point where they have some power to work, but not quite enough to really fly away."

They walked back carefully from the deep hidden stream into the wider entrance to the cave.

Bess stared at the strange insect-like space ship. It was definitely longer than she imagined. She had only seen the circular saucers that had chased her across the prairie in the night. This looked almost antique in comparison. Like something from old Buck Rogers or Flash Gordon serials from twenty years ago. "I see what you mean about calling this a bus," she said as she stared in the tiny windows, crammed with seats.

"I think this thing is older than we realize," her father said cryptically.

"Don't these run on uranium?" The moon men had stolen uranium from a mine on the Trulys' property when they tried to start their invasion to power their ships.

"Well, yes, kind of," Steve scratched his head on the subject. It was a little beyond him. He understood the notions of flight, and the power of both propeller and jet engines, but nuclear energy was his wife's skill. "They make power that way, but they seem to charge batteries, and then, you remember, they actually run on the gravity, or repelling the gravity, from the surface."

Bess remembered how the saucers had struggled with the heavy gravity of the Earth compared to the moon.

"This thing was just charged by electricity, and then they used something like a catapult, or even like what we use with the Starlighter, to launch. It was like they blasted off, then used the power of the ship, and the Earth's gravity, to pull them here. They used up the last of the electricity to land."

"And what about those things?" she pointed at the backpacks they wore.

"These? Yeah, pretty neat, huh. They work in a similar way. These things," he pointed at the joints on his knees, where big knobs rotated as he walked, "are like your little generator. It gives just a little charge to make the pack work. Then you press here," he held out a button on a cable, "and then the pads on your feet sense when you jump, and these things," Steve swung around, trying to point out two silver circles on the backpack, like strange jet nozzles, "give a push against gravity. You can jump up about fifty feet or more, depending on how much you weigh. Then it senses the ground when you get close and cushions your landing."

"So it's not like a jetpack, right?"

"No, it's more a," Steve thought, "jump pack."

Bess wanted to try it, but now was not the time, especially inside a cave.

"So it was one of you I saw from the mountain yesterday!" It suddenly dawned on her what she had seen.

"Probably," Steve agreed.

"Well, look, kiddo, all this may seem like fun, but we really need to get out of here, sooner rather than later. We don't know if those moon men are hot on our trail or not. You are going to have to head back and get help here as soon as you can. I hope Electra is well rested, it may mean a long day's ride for her."

"Gosh, Dad, I don't even know if I can get back the way I came. The path down was awful steep. Any chance we can go the other way?" She began getting her map out.

"Maybe, it's a longer distance, but..."

Just then, lights came on in the cavern. The space ship from the moon began to light up, humming with life. It had gotten enough power to start back up.

Then a bright light came on the top, blinking like a lighthouse and as bright as a landing light. The people standing around the cave shielded their eyes.

Then, they heard the sound. A loud and monotonous beeping came from somewhere inside the space ship.

Two of the refugees began to frantically climb up to the ship, prying open the cockpit. "It's the location marker!" one screamed. "They found us!"

CHAPTER 9


Let Electra Fly


"What do we do?!"

It was a desperate cry from one of the refugees. Most stood around, looking at each other, or the two men who crawled into the ship, or Steve and Bess. Four of them ran outside and immediately jumped off the cliffside. They were going to warn the rest of their group.

"Disconnect it!" yelled one man at the other inside the cockpit. Bess presumed they were the pilots.

"No, they already know our location! We have to move the ship!" answered the other. The rest seemed frozen in fear.

"We need to stop that signal!" Bess yelled.

"They're right," Steve corrected her. "If we just turn it off, they may already know where we are."

"Can you at least turn off that beeping?!" Bess yelled up to the two pilots. One reached over to try to find some control to the sound. The other pulled a tool from his belt and looked around until he found the speaker blaring the horn sound, then he jammed it in until the sound stopped.

"Well, that's a way to do it," Bess said. "At least we can think now."

Bess had taken a lot of abilities from both her parents. She got her adventurous side from her father, so she was willing to take needed risks and run toward danger when needed. But she got her intelligence from her mother, who solved problems by both figuring them out, and removing all the possibilities that wouldn't give her the right results. Bess, on less stressful times than this, referred to her mother as "Sherlock Holmes" for the way she solved mysteries.

Bess did it, too, but she needed a moment of relative quiet.

"Okay, we can't turn it off, can we fly the ship out? Take it somewhere else?"

"Not enough power to get far enough away, and the Starlighter still can't move. It would take hours."

"So, we can't move the saucer," she just gave in and called the space ship that, since she didn't have time to figure out a better word, "And we can't turn it off." She stopped, silent, for a few seconds. One of the pilots took a breath in, but Steve held up his hand to wait. Bess would find a solution.

"So, we just move the saucer, anyway," She decided firmly.

"We just said we can't do that," Steve responded.

"No, we make them *think* we've moved it. We just move the transponder." Bess smiled a thin but proud smile. "We remove it, working, and take it away. Make the moon men, sorry," she nodded at the two pilots. They were "moon men," too, but they weren't the ones she was concerned with right now. "We make the other moon men think it's flying away. We take it out, I'll ride it out on Electra, as far as possible, and hide it somewhere deep in the woods. It will give us time to get them away from here, at least."

"But how to do we power it without disconnecting it from the battery?" asked one of the pilots.

Bess thought for another second, then snapped her fingers with an idea. She dug into her bag and pulled out her spare power pack for her Zap-Gun. "Will this do?"

A hurried twenty minutes later, and Bess was down the hill and on Electra. She had decided to go back the way she came, because she knew the land better. There would be fewer surprises, and more places for her to hide.

Bess didn't know how long before the moon men came down from space. They must have been close, in a relative sense. Close when it came to space travel could be 10,000 miles. But then, she also didn't know how fast the space ship would travel.

Bess rode Electra at a gallop, leaning into the wind as it blew against her face. Electra flew over the open flat lands, and jumped over obstacles like they were barely there. She was in her element as a fast prairie horse, excited and ready to please Bess. Horses had a sense for their riders, and Bess and Electra had a special bond. They had already been through a lot. This was pure joy for the horse.

Bess was more worried. She had time to think, and wonder. "Would they send another giant space ship, something huge to level the entire mountainside?" The last time, the moon men had torn holes in the earth and blown the sides of mountains down. Bess could only hope this would be a less violent encounter.

She let herself relax, loosening the reins, and letting Electra fly. The horse's ears fell back, and she began to pant with the exertion. Bess felt Electra's pace pick up even more. They didn't know where they were going, but that made it even more fun. It was just an adventure, what Bess's horse had needed for days after boring slow rides around the ranch.

Bess had to decide when to stop and rest. It took much less time now to get back to her camp site from the night before. She recognized the grassy meadow and the small stream. She even spotted her telltale campfire. It was a bare patch of sand and white ash.

"No time for camping now," Bess thought. "I have to find a place to hide this thing, and then get out of sight." Bess rode to the north, while Steve helped to lead the refugees to safety. She had given the map to him, and marked the possible spots where they may meet up on her handkerchief.

A quick stop let Electra drink and graze, while Bess scouted the path forward with her binoculars. She decided to find a very rocky spot, not too high, but as far away as she could from the path she had followed down the day before. She wanted a tough place for the moon men to land. "Make 'em walk," she said to herself. "They don't have horses." Then she wondered if they would also have those jump packs that the others had escaped with. That would make things worse for her.

It was a quick stop, and Bess was back on Electra. This time, the land was more open, and she could see where she was going easily, back toward the rugged cliffs of the Brokeoff Mountains. In her backpack, she felt the warmth of the transponder. She wondered if she could feel it buzzing, vibrating, louder, even though the warning siren was disconnected. Or was it just her imagination spurring her on faster?

Bess finally reached the base of the cliffs. Far off to her right, she saw where she had come down the mountainside of the plateau, where she had seen the *bruja*, which turned out to be her father, "maybe a *brujo,*" she figured, the male equivalent. The way those things flew was a bit like magic.

Bess shook the thought out of her head and got to work. Leaving Electra at the bottom of the hillside, she began to scramble up the cliff. Instead of searching around, she simply found a small alcove and shoved the transponder in it, still attached to her spare power pack.

Bess scrambled down the hill, got on Electra, and rode away, as fast as she could.

## CHAPTER 10

Strangers Visit

Bess hid as far away as she could get, while still able to see where she had hidden the transponder. Tucked into the woods that bordered the two natural park areas, she unsaddled Electra to let her rest and graze. It could be moments, it could be hours or a day. If it started to get very dark, Bess wasn't sure what she would do. There was no way to find her way back in the dark. Bess was not going to turn on her Zap-Gun in case the moon men in the space ship showed up and saw her in the darkness. She wasn't about to lead them back when she had worked so hard to lead them away.

So she hid and waited.

Bess was near where she originally had come down the plateau. She didn't want to go out in the open, even if the skies were clear, just in case the space ship they all feared would show up suddenly. She looked at the trail with her binoculars.

"It would be a lot harder, and slower, to get back up that way, if we even could," she whispered to Electra, who wasn't listening as she ate her way through some soft grass. "I wish I had another carrot for you, girl, I'm sorry. But hopefully we can get out of here soon."

That was one of many problems Bess had. She ticked them off in her head. There were places to hide to the south, and it looked like a cut in the mountains near an old cabin that was used by a prospector at some time in the last century. But that would take time, maybe days, to move that many people, even if they started today. She had to get back as quickly as possible to help, but also to alert her father that the space ship had arrived. She had to do that while not being detected by the moon men. She had to do *that* in the daylight, because moving at night would be slow and dangerous.

She also needed to eat. Bess had packed enough food for several days, but most of it involved heating up water in a pan. Electra could eat oats dry, but Bess needed them cooked. She had fortunately packed a packet of peanuts and some beef jerky, a popular trail snack for cowgirls like her. "If only I had a Coke," she complained. There were no ice cream stands or soda shops in the middle of nowhere.

Bess wondered what her friends were doing now. Lydia would be getting off work soon, Aurora probably came home the same day Bess left, and Jesse would be working at the ice cream shop, with its own air conditioning and cool, cool, treats. Bess could taste the wild tropical treats that Jesse's father made, with coconut or pineapple in the ice cream. Then her mouth watered as she thought about how the ice cream cones at the end of the snack would make her thirsty and want to drink a glass of ice water, dripping with condensation, sticking to a thin white paper napkin.

Her jerky was poor in comparison. She gnawed at it with a vengeful bite.

Minutes ticked by into an hour. Bess looked at the sky. Most of the day had been spent riding, and now the sun began to fall lower in the sky. The shade of the trees kept her hidden, but the sun beat through with summer heat. Bess took off her boots to cool her feet. That was another problem. She needed rest, as did Electra. She needed to get her boots off, and Electra needed her saddle off. But if the moon people came, she would have to leave quickly. That wouldn't be easy barefoot and bare back.

She was also getting tired. It had been a long day. She had found her father, only to have to ride away from him. Now she felt herself getting drowsy. "Just a little nap," her brain told her, "you'll know if a giant space ship appears..."

Bess felt herself being to nod off. The warmth of the day combined with a long, long ride, and not sleeping well the night before had all taken its toll on her. Her eyes closed and opened, closed...

She awoke five minutes later, startled, not by any loud noise or strange thing in the sky, but by something that seemed to catch her attention while she slept. Like people talking and singing.

Bess struggled to wake herself up, to get her eyes fully opened. She rubbed them and took a drink of water, then poured some on a bandanna to rub on her face. She was sure she must have been dreaming.

Then she heard it again.

Looking around, she saw a strange shape coming down the path where she had been the day before. Then another, and another.

Bess jumped up, awake, and began to put her boots on.

"C'mon, Electra! We gotta move!"

# CHAPTER 11

## Found!

Bess had to hurry. Everything could be ruined if she didn't get on Electra and out of her hiding place. If the space ship came over now, things would be so much worse.

She kicked at her boots. "Ugh," she struggled as one folded over her ankle, "I don't have time for this!" She pulled it off and tried again.

Once she had her boots on, she picked up her saddle and lugged it over to Electra, who stopped grazing when she saw Bess coming. Electra stood still as Bess threw the saddle on her. "Sorry, girl," Bess took a moment to stroke the horse's neck. She didn't mean to be rough. With a quick pull of the cinch, Electra was as ready as she could be on a moment's notice. Bess pulled on the saddle horn and gave a tug to the stirrups to see if the saddle moved, then leapt upon Electra. She grabbed the reins and with a soft kick and cluck, the two were off.

Bess recognized the shapes she had seen immediately. She galloped out of the woods and into the open, about two hundred yards from the bottom of the trail she had used. She saw the strange shapes almost at the bottom of the trail, going slowly so they didn't slip. Bess pulled her Zap-Gun out with a spin from its holster, and dialed the setting down with a quick snap. Then she held it into the air, high above her, and squeezed the trigger. The blue light glowed into the vanishing twilight. It was bright and cold compared to the warm oranges and yellows of the setting sun. She would be seen and noticed almost immediately.

She hoped.

Bess wondered if she was rushing for nothing. She had hurried so fast to hide the transponder, and then waited in the woods so far away, that she had fallen asleep when all the stress and worry fell off of her once she was able to relax for a moment.

Then this.

This was a surprise. This was not what she expected. She had waited, unsure and in fear. She had pictured a big lumbering space ship like she had seen before, a month ago. It had stormed out of the morning sky breathing smoke and rocks from its strange engines powered by the Earth's own gravity. Bess was sure a similar one would show up and blot out the sky and she would have absolutely no idea how to stop it.

She had not expected three stumbling shapes coming down a nearly hidden hill.

How had they found her?

How had they found their way this far, to end up only a quarter of a mile away, and she was closing fast, her Zap-Gun up and at the ready.

She turned up her Zap-Gun a notch, and pulled the trigger hard, pouring power into the discharge barrel. It lit up like a spotlight. It was a fast moving blue lighthouse on top of a flying horse, ridden by a wild strawberry blond cowgirl in the middle of a wild and forbidding forest.

The three shapes stopped. They had seen her, riding wild and with abandon.

Bess rode at a fast gallop, then, with only feet between them, she drew Electra up short, pulling hard on the reins. Her horse dug in with her shoes. Bess pressed her feet into the stirrups and leaned back hard, to keep her from being thrown over the head of Electra and tumbling into the sharp gravel at the horse's feet.

Finally stopped, Bess lifted her head. She stared at what she saw.

Three riders, three people on three horses, all stared at her in wonder and surprise.

Bess beamed at them, with the same feeling, as one then another spoke to her.

"Bess! We found you!"

# CHAPTER 12

## Stealing All The Wishes

Bess stared in wonder, smiling even though she was worried about all the things that could be happening any moment. Sitting on the three horses were her best friends, Lydia, Aurora, and Jesse, all laughing and stunned to have Bess ride up to them out of nowhere.

"Where did you come from?" asked Jesse, as he stared at the woods in the distance. Bess had just popped up out of nowhere.

"Where did *I* come from?!" Bess answered. "Where did *you* come from? What are you doing here?!"

"We came to help you!" Lydia responded.

"Yeah, I got back home the morning after you left," Aurora said. "We found out you came down here to look for your father. Joel told us when we went over to your house." Joel was the other foreman for the C Bar M, along with Manny. "What? You couldn't wait a day for your friends to come with you?"

Jesse laughed, "She's probably already found him, knowing Bess. Any luck?"

"Well, yes," Bess said. For a moment, relief flooded through her. As she told her friends about finding her father, that he was well, all the work and tiredness poured out of her and she started to slouch in the saddle. Bess was tired. With her friends there, people she could count on, she felt a bit of pressure come off her shoulders. "I'm so glad you came. How did you get here?"

Aurora waved at Jesse. "This guy borrowed a truck and took my dad's trailer. We loaded up our horses, and one for Cowboy Jesse here." Jesse was a well known hot rodder in town. He owned an orange jalopy he affectionately called his Desert Cadillac. But there were no roads and no way to drive it out into this rocky wilderness. Bess looked at Jesse, who seemed uncomfortable on a horse instead of behind a steering wheel.

"One horsepower," he patted the neck of his ride, a beautiful brown and white paint horse that was a colorful twin to Aurora's black and white ride. Lydia's golden palomino blended into the earthy colors and Lydia's ecru summer riding clothes.

Bess wanted to get off Electra and hug them each by the neck, but she realized there was so much to do. "Quick," she said, as she looked at the darkening sky, "We need to get back under some cover. I'll explain more when we are away from here." Bess shook her head in disbelief. She was still stunned to have her friends with her. Now she felt like everything would be better. She just needed time. An hour or a night, or even just a moment.

Once she got under the cover of some tall trees and their green canopy of leaves, she felt like she could stop. They needed to know what was going on, besides the fact that she had found her father.

"Okay, what's your story, morning glory?" asked Lydia.

Bess would normally answer with "What's your tale, nightingale!" but she didn't. Her friends knew that there was something serious going on and all stopped smiling. They were going to pay special attention to Bess now.

"Listen, you're not going to believe this," she started. "Our friends from the moon are back."

Aurora let out a quiet gasp, and Jesse frowned. They all remembered the last time those *friends* showed up.

"But there's a lot more to it, see." Bess explained how the families had escaped from the moon and were on the run, how Steve had found them and helped hide them. Then she got to the transponder.

"It's hidden right over," Bess tried to point it out, but the sky had darkened so much, and she had ridden back and forth, that she didn't know exactly where she had hidden it. "Oh, shoot, I'm not sure. But that doesn't matter. The outlaws could be coming over the hill any time. The signal went out," she tried to figure out how long it had been, seven, eight hours ago? "Around noon, I guess. I've been going all day, honestly, I have no sense of what time it is, or when they may show up. I was scared they would come blasting out of space when we were in the open just now."

Bess thought of one thing she needed to tell them. "Look," she pulled out her handkerchief, "Look here. There's a rocky outcropping and a hidden cave. That's where they were. But they are going to this point here." She pointed out a mark on the map. "In case the outlaws," Bess was now comfortable with the word for the bad moon men, to differentiate them from the families that escaped the moon, "don't stop. You need to know where to go to help them."

"We will all help them, don't worry," Lydia leaned over to put her hand on Bess's shoulder. "We took care of those goons before, we can handle them again. This is our element," she waved her hand into the darkness, "and they won't know where to go."

"Yup," Jesse agreed. He reached up over his shoulder. While the other girls each had a Zap-Gun on their hips, Jesse always carried a folding shovel to dig out of the sand in case he got stuck. He patted it with a menacing smile. "Anyone messes with us, they get the business end of my desert crowbar!"

"So, what do we do now?" Aurora asked. "You look whupped, Bess. Should we wait here and see what shows up? Or do we start heading back? It's getting dark."

"Yeah," Bess agreed. "You have been riding for a while, and poor Electra has been going all day. She could use a night's rest. Or just another couple hours. Who knows? Maybe the moon outlaws won't even show up." She tried to delude herself. But the transponder had been turned on. She knew those bandits would be looking for the escaped outcasts.

"Did you have a plan after this?" Jesse asked.

"No, we were kind of winging it," Bess admitted. "I just wanted to get that marker beacon away from those people. After that, well, I guess I'm open to ideas."

"Look," Lydia spoke up, "We're all tired, you especially. We have a lot of food," she patted her saddle bags, "Let's find a good place far away from here and set up a camp. If they come, we'll see them. If not, well, we can set off early in the morning. A good rest will clear our heads, especially yours, Bess."

Everyone agreed, and Bess took them to a small grassy clearing with a heavy grove of trees that would provide a thick hiding place, along with grazing area for the horses. They unsaddled their rides and tied them to stakes. Bess let Electra go free. She would stay with the other horses for safety without being tied up. Bess knew Electra needed a moment to stretch and jump, as well as sleep.

"Should be start a fire?" Lydia asked.

Bess didn't want to have a blazing glow that would shine like a beacon up into the sky at night. Even a tiny fire would show up like a spotlight in the dark woodlands. But she was hungry, tired, and needed the security of seeing her friends in the light. They had brought food to cook, not just dried beans and bread. Her stomach fought against her brain, and the stomach won easily.

"Let's just not build it really high, and we can have a pan of water nearby to douse it quickly," she said.

With that, the four teens settled in to a more comfortable night together in the woods than they would have had alone. Aurora cooked fluffy tortillas in a pan while Jesse heated up rice, beans, and chicken from a can. "I'm just glad you didn't bring that whole chicken in a can thing," Lydia pretended to gag at the idea of an entire chicken in a big tin can. She pulled bags of M&Ms out of her satchel as a dessert treat. Bess ate hers with relish. She had left so fast she didn't think of packing the sweet treat that could handle the warm weather. Bess only had a bag of peanuts.

The four of them laid down on the grass near the smoldering embers of the fire, staring up at the stars of a dark sky through the filter of leaves of the trees overhead. Bess was stretched out on her bedroll. Even with the trees and the mountain ranges around her, she was surprised at just how clear and dark the night was. She was used to the big open skies, but back home there was always a glow from civilization, the warm brown tungsten color of the lights of town, or the bright green and red landing lights that marked her airstrip like a Christmas tree. Here, there was no light for miles. Nothing on the horizon, no cities pumping out their streetlights, not even a plane going over. The stars shone like dots, with no points. When she watched long enough, Bess would catch a stray meteor streaking across the sky. "This would be a great place to look for shooting stars," Bess said. There was a big meteor shower coming up soon. When they didn't have to worry and wonder about the events of the day, a trip out to the Brokeoff Mountains would be fun for her and her friends.

"I don't know about you," Aurora let out a soft yawn, "but I can barely stay awake." She wiggled her feet. "Woo, my tootsies, they are happy to be out of those boots." The rest agreed, all putting their feet in the air and waving them, laughing at how ridiculous they looked, and glad no one could see them.

"I think we should all get some sleep," Jesse agreed. "Do you want me to stay up? Keep an eye out? I don't know if we would hear anything or not. We can take turns. Bess, you can sleep through. You've earned it."

Bess didn't argue. She looked up at the sky, at the stars so far away. Only a month ago, they seemed so distant that she couldn't imagine them as more than bright dots. Now she had to worry about strange evil men from the moon coming to her home. She shook the thought out of her mind. Tonight, she had some others to help her worry. Hopefully, she could get some sleep.

Bess fell quickly into a deep slumber, only to be awakened just as fast. The dark sky was still there, the leaves quivered softly in an invisible breeze. She rubbed her eyes to open them better. It was dark all around. She could smell the sour pungent smell of the fire and hear a crackling steam. Someone had poured water on it recently to put it out, and now the air was filled with an acidic dry ash smell, the opposite of the woody smell of logs burning.

Someone was shaking her roughly, trying to wake her up. Someone called her name quietly, "Bess... Bess, wake up."

Bess finally got her eyes open clearly. She looked up at the sky, still dark, just as she had seen. But something was missing.

"Where are the stars?!"

CHAPTER 13

Closing The Front Door

The sky should have been filled with stars, but it was a dark and blank canvas through the trees. Bess felt like her eyes still weren't focusing. She had a strange humming in her ears.

Then she saw lights, finally, like a strange green sunrise moving quickly through the leaves. She was so tired, she knew something was wrong, but her fuzzy brain wasn't processing what was happening. Something seemed familiar, and bad. Lydia was shaking her shoulder.

"Bess, Bess!" it was a shouted whisper, "Wake up! They're here!"

She realized what was happening then. Just over their heads was a space ship, slowly hovering toward the cliffside, big, round, ugly, glowing with a soft green light. "Have they found us?!" Bess almost yelled, then caught herself, then realized it was unlikely the moon men would be able to hear or see them from above.

Jesse stood over the fire with an empty pan and canteen. He shoveled vigorously to cover the last of the embers so no one would see the telltale fire. "I don't think so, they just appeared over that northern ridge. They circled over the woods and are heading to where you pointed out you hid the transponder. As soon as I saw it, I dumped out water on the fire and started waking you up. What do we do?"

Bess was already pulling on her boots. "We need to see them. If they stop and get out, I want to know how many of them there are. And I want to see this ship they have." She stared up at the sky. The big saucer had passed over by now and Bess could see the stars clearly. "It's different than those little ones we saw. I need to know if we can stop it somehow.

"Lydia, can you stay here and saddle the horses? We need to get riding as soon as we know what we're dealing with," Bess asked.

"Sure," Lydia already grabbed Jesse's saddle. "I don't want to get close to that thing if I don't have to." Lydia had helped to bring down a moon saucer with Bess once, but she had little desire to get close to one again.

"Great, Jesse, you and Aurora come with me." Bess already felt confident knowing her friends were with her.

The three teens walked carefully through the woods. The darkness was a double edged sword. It hid their movements from anyone who might be watching, but it made moving fast difficult. Branches and tree roots reached out in the dark to trip and grab at them, making every step in the inky dark treacherous. The big saucer gleamed green and ugly off to the northwest. It was a lighthouse of ominous portent, a warning that instead of driving sailors away from a dangerous shore, called Bess and her friends closer to the danger and risk. Like a moth to a hot burning flame, the three moved closer and closer to the light, in hopes of seeing what the light will show, unaware of how they may get burned.

Jesse grunted as he took a tumble, and Bess got whipped by a mesquite branch. Aurora, usually the most riskiest and most curious of the bunch, somehow came out unscathed. They walked into a small clearing that opened to a rocky dry bed of sand and stone. "Just when we need the cover," Jesse said.

The big ship was hovering over the cliff face, but there was no place nearby to land. The entire area was either strewn with boulders that had rolled off the ridge long ago, or covered with trees and brush. Bess was thinking that they may open a hatch and jump out. "I wonder if they have those jump packs like Dad does," Bess thought.

The ship hovered over the ground, about a hundred feet up. The rocks rumbled and vibrated.

The engines from the big saucer shook the earth, using its own gravity against itself to lift the ship. Bess could see bits of debris floating in the intakes above the ship, which would find their way off to the sides to rain down on the metal and bounce off. It was such a strange technology. Bess took her eyes off the engines to focus on her task. The moon outlaws had found the transponder, but they haven't gotten out yet. "Maybe they can't," she thought. "I don't think they can get out, with all that thrust there," she told Jesse and Aurora. "There's no place to land. That's why I put it there."

"Well," Aurora said, "Knowing these dudes, they'll find a way."

"I wonder if there is a way to stop them," Jesse said. "I wish we could send them back to the moon."

Bess thought for a second. She knew that they were already at a disadvantage, with just four of them, three Zap-Guns, and no support form anyone else. No one even knew where they were. "We can't do anything," she decided. "We need to see what we're dealing with, and then get out of here. It's going to be slow going, but we have to get back and tell Dad they are here. He'll think of something." Bess then thought about how she would have to find her father, again, along with all the refugees. "One problem at a time," she said. If she got distracted from the issue at hand, in front of her, she would miss something important.

The ship started to move. Aurora grabbed Bess by the shoulder holding her closer for a moment, then letting go. "Sorry, it startled me," she said.

"They're looking for a place to park," Bess said.

"They *found* one," Jesse answered. He pointed up into the darkness.

The cliff began to glow as the ship rose. There was no place nearby to put a ship that big. "Where?" Bess asked.

"There," Jesse pointed into the lightening ridge.

The plateau where Bess had first stopped to scout for her father stood out, gleaming in the dirty green light of the space ship. It was easily wide enough to handle the entire craft.

They watched as the big ship maneuvered over the flat landing area. As it got close to the ground, a huge dust storm blew up underneath. Rocks and dirt flew away from the open landing spot, and small scrub brush was pulled up by the roots to fly off in desert snowballs of black and brown. The little tumbleweeds went soaring into the darkness. When it got within ten feet of the plateau, the sides of the cliff began to break and crumble from the pressure of the gravity waves. The side of the cliff gave way, sending rocks down in an avalanche. Then the side of the hill was covered in a dark dust, obscuring the damage.

It extended four large hinged landing legs and settled with a heavy, dusty plop. Even from the distance, the three teens heard the distinct whine of the saucer's engines settling down.

It took only moments for hatches to open, and the outlaw moon men piled out. Bess pulled her binoculars from her pack to see them up close. They looked familiar, in a bad way. Dressed in black, with tight hoods over their heads. Bess knew they were some type of helmet, and the clothes were thick and hot. She half saw, half pictured their pale white skin and dark circles around their eyes. They looked like horrifying ghouls from a Halloween party, only they were real, and worse than any ghoul.

A group of them stared down the cliff, along the far edge near where the transponder was buried. There was no easy way down, and it would only be harder in the dark. The moon men didn't do well in the dark. Here in the southern desert mountains, it was nothing but dark.

Until one of them lit up a giant burning white light and tossed it down the cliff face.

The three of them watched the bright light fall. "It's a devil's sparkler," Aurora gasped in awe. It even lit them up for a moment. They all ducked into the now distinct shadows cast by the light. Two more were lit, sending huge white flames in spurts of fire and sparks above them.

"It's magnesium," Jesse said, shielding his eyes. "It burns real bright. It'll burn under water, it's so hot."

With the way lit, the teens could see clearly what the outlaws' plan was. Two moon men tossed a big cable down the side of the cliff and began to use it to walk down the side toward the transponder.

"They'll find it soon enough," Bess said.

"Bess..." Jesse tapped her on the shoulder,

"I just want to see if they find it."

"Bess..." Jesse became insistent.

"Just a few more minutes," she asked as she stared intently at the outlaws climbing down the hill.

"BESS!" Jesse shook her.

"What?!" Bess had been concentrating so hard on the moon men that she barely noticed Jesse calling her.

"Look!" Jesse pointed up toward the saucer, glowing but still on the ledge.

The bright white light of the magnesium flares had lit the cliffside to almost daylight. The edge of the plateau had cracked and tumbled to a sheer face. All of the narrow path that Bess and her friends had used to get down was now gone, replaced by jagged razor lines of rock, straight up hundreds of feet to the plateau.

"Well," Bess said, resigned, "We aren't getting out that way."

## CHAPTER 14

Into The Forest

"Yep, that's it, we gotta go."

Bess stood up and began to move quickly back to their campsite. Saddles or no saddles, they needed to get going, now. There was no going back that way. She needed to lead her father and all the rest out of the desert and into civilization. If she had to, she would go buy sets of clothes for all of them and just put them on a bus to the ranch. "Just let those outlaws try and find'em." Now, if only she could get that far.

A few scratches and bumps later, they finally came upon the small clearing where Lydia waited in the starry darkness with four horses saddled and loaded with their packs. "Poor Electra," Bess took a moment to coo over her hard working horse, "This is a lot for you and me both, isn't it, girl?" Electra whinnied a soft answer, but stood tall and still, tense, ready to run. She sensed danger and was waiting to help Bess as soon as she climbed into the saddle.

"Which way do we go?" asked Lydia.

"That way," Bess said assuredly. No time for plotting a path at night, and no way to turn on a light. It would be a slow step by step trip in the night. But every step would be one step closer, one step sooner, to be away from the outlaws and closer to where her father waited.

They all moved, with Bess in the lead. She was just going in the direction she knew. The sun would rise early, and she would get a better idea of where she needed to go once it was brighter.

It was hours of tiring slow riding. Sometimes they got off the horses and led them through thick brushy sections. Bess risked a soft and quick shine with her Zap-Gun. She hoped that the flying saucer and moon men were far behind her. She could only hope and wish that they would stay where they were, at least until daybreak.

Bess wondered if the moon men could read her mind from far away. They were strange and mysterious people.

She wondered that because as soon as she wished they would stay put, she heard a distant crash of sound. Looking back behind her, through an opening in the trees, she could see the stars over the silhouette of the edge of the Brokeoff Mountains. Just above the front edge, she saw the distinct glowing green of the moon space ship. They had lifted off.

"Great, that's all we need," Aurora said. "Come down here and I'll knock you down with a rock." The rest of the teens believed she could do it, with one throw. They all felt the same way.

"They don't know where we are, do they?" Asked Lydia.

"They don't know we are out here," Bess said. "They only know now that the refugees know someone is looking for them, and that the transponder was hidden, or moved. They probably will start looking nearby. Those moon goons don't know about us or our horses."

The space ship far up in the sky behind them only heightened their tension, which made the four pick up the pace on their horses. They were fortunate to find a small section of open ground covered with mostly grass, which allowed them to travel at a slow trot. Another big forest awaited them. Bess could see her goal in the far distance, the ragged pointy cliffs of the Guadalupe Mountains. From there she cold find her way across the streams, trees, and foothills, to where her father should be. The four teens purposefully didn't look back. Looking back would only confirm their fears if the ship was closer, and only heighten their anxiety.

If it was gone, they would just wonder where it went.

So they looked forward. They moved forward.

It only took another half hour for them all to give in. They heard a terrible crunching sound from far off, like thick cloth being torn. Or an earthquake. It was such a strange mix of tearing and rending that the four of them could not identify it.

Bess and the others stopped, wheeled their horses and looked. The ship was still far off, but closer now, and moving. It hovered over the ground, not high in the sky. The saucer was slowly zig-zagging its way across the the last copse of trees. With the green energy pouring out of the engines, they could see what was happening, even from afar. The ship was flying over the trees, as if it was scanning for the escaped refugees. But as it passed over each section of land, the big powerful gravity beams tore into the forest, toppling trees and ripping soil up from the floor.

"Oh, no," Lydia gasped.

"They're tearing the forest out," Bess gasped the words out from near breathless lungs. She had seen this before, but not to this extent. The smaller saucers had cut holes in the prairie, but this was destruction on a much higher level. Trees flew up from the roots, dirt clouded the green light, turning it a dirty olive color. The ship just moved from spot to spot, stopping as if it looked for something, then moving on. In its wake it left nothing but the destruction of trees and dirt.

"Oh, the poor birds," Lydia gaped at the saucer as it pulled up the trees by the roots. Any animals there would probably be awakened by the horrible noise, but the birds asleep in the trees would find their world in a tumble, if they woke up at all before the branches were stripped and broken.

Bess felt terrible. There was no way to stop them. If they got too close, the horses and riders would be sucked up just as easily as everything else. "We have to get moving. If they find us, things will get worse quick."

The riders had an open spot, and they turned their horses toward the woods at a gallop. Again, it felt like the saucer knew their thoughts, as it seemed to speed up, too. Only it could cover more distance in the air than the teens could cover on the ground. The rumbling destruction only got closer and closer.

By the time they reached the woods, the saucer was close enough that they could make out detaisl. "Are they after us?!" Lydia cried.

"If they were, they would go straight toward us," Jesse said.

"It doesn't help any if they still are coming in our direction!" Bess yelled. They felt yet another rumble. "This forest is taller trees, I remember it. Light it up, we need to go fast!" Bess drew her Zap-Gun with one hand while holding the reins with the other. With a squeeze of the trigger, a bright blue light opened up the way in front of her. Within a second, two more beams lit up the woods.

"Go straight!" Bess yelled. By now the saucer was close enough to hear. The rumble became a crushing sound of trees being pulled up and rocks being tossed in loud thumps. They weren't even using their strange and destructive ray beam. It was just the energy from the engines. The horses picked up the pace. A scrape from a tree branch was less of a risk than being tossed into the sky from those huge gravity thrusters.

The next pass was nearer still. It cut a line across the last bit of forest behind them. Then a cloud of sand and soil went up from where they had just been. It hid the ship at first. As the teens looked over their shoulders, they saw the saucer emerge from the dust cloud as a green monstrous disc, with its blunt leading edge rolling away the clouds with its rounded wedge.

"They're getting closerrrr...!" Jesse had a bit of panic in his voice. He wasn't as good on his horse, and was worried about what to do if he couldn't outrun the destruction.

Another huge dig into the ground, as the ship turned and headed back in the opposite direction. The ship was cutting diagonal lines in the land, like it was unzipping the earth.

"We can't outrun it!" Bess wasn't going to let her friends get hurt from these outlaws. Another huge cut, even closer, crushed down behind them. They picked up their speed to a sprint, faster than a gallop. The horses snorted and whinnied, terrified by the sights behind them. They could see almost all around them, and they responded with fear at any threat from behind. This was a most deadly predator. It was one they had never seen before.

The ship turned, this time really pushing into the curve as it shot out dirt and debris far into the night. It was close enough that the green glow started to light up in front of them. Bess and the other girls turned their Zap-Guns off and took the reins with both hands. They didn't need any light anymore.

"We can't get caught in that exhaust!" yelled Jesse. The sound of rocks and trees being pulled up was loud enough that they had to shout. He tried to turn his horse away from the oncoming blast. Lydia was next to him, and followed his direction. Bess and Aurora were moving faster, getting ahead. Bess was going to turn the opposite direction and hopefully outrace the space ship as it went one way and they went another. She looked behind her, and saw only Aurora at her heels, keeping up at high speed. Jesse and Lydia were now getting farther off, with the space ship coming up fast between them.

The ship turned again, cutting another deep gouge into the earth as it changed direction.

Then it started its unstoppable run across the ground, throwing trees, bushes, rocks and sand into the air.

Jesse and Lydia were right in the middle of its path.

# CHAPTER 15

## Emeralds In The Leaves

Bess saw Jesse pull up on the reins of his horse, while Lydia turned to her left and began to race away from the ship. It looked like the saucer was chasing after her, and the flying saucer was winning easily.

Bess had turned to the right, hoping to get away from the ship. Aurora and Bess were going to run directly away from the direction of the saucer, in hopes of getting past where it would turn before it came back. Then they would just follow it at a distance.

She hadn't planned on getting separated. And worse, Jesse was caught somewhere in the path of the saucer's engines, and Lydia was being chased down second by second.

The two teens and their horses would be picked up and tossed like the trees in the air. The saucer would be throwing them around like a child with an unwanted toy. Bess wished she could go faster, but she was already pushing Electra to her limit. The poor horse panted with the exertion. She foamed and snorted as she tried to go faster at the willing of her rider.

Aurora and her horse moved ahead of Bess. Aurora's ride was a little less tired, and very fast when tight turns were needed. Aurora rode past Bess and kept going. Their lives were on the line, as well as the lives of their friends. They had to get back to Jesse and Lydia, to find them and see if they were hurt, injured, or worse.

Aurora got past where the saucer had made its last turn. She pulled out her Zap-Gun and lit the way. The saucer carried on with its work, oblivious to the damage and destruction it had caused.

Where the saucer had turned was a huge rut, covered with rocks and brush. It was if an impassible wall had been built around the huge tear in the earth. Bess and Aurora kept circling around, heading farther backwards to where they had been before. They finally got around the turn, and the land there was less mangled with deep cuts. Two lines, about six feet deep and four feet wide, were burned into the land. "We have to find them," Aurora said, her voice cracking with worry. "We might be able to get across here."

"Look!" Bess shown her Zap-Gun farther down the destroyed land. "There, it's more of an indent, not two big ravines." The land was flatter, and they probably could walk their horses over, or at least get off the horses and walk. There was a huge tree on its side that lay in the middle of the rut. Branches stuck out from brush that had been caught up in it, with only about a ten foot opening.

Suddenly, like a wild beast pouncing at them, a huge shape jumped over the only opening in the fallen tree.

Bess turned off her Zap-Gun, snapped the power up, and aimed at the thing. She didn't know if it was a bear stirred by the destruction, or could it be a moon man jumping out to attack.

"Wait!" a voice called, "It's just me!" Lydia lit up her own Zap-Gun with a pale blue light high over her head. In the dark, Lydia's horse had leapt over the only opening she could find in between the torn land and the outside prairie.

"Thank goodness you're alright!" yelled Aurora. "You are alright, aren't you? Are you hurt?"

"I'm good, a little scared, that's for sure," Lydia talked a bit louder than she needed to. "And maybe a bit deafened. That thing was loud."

"Where's Jesse?" Bess asked. She hoped he hadn't been caught up in the gravity beams of that saucer.

"He's fine," Lydia said. "He actually came and saved me. Pulled me out of the path of that thing right before it got to me. He's a little mad, but other than that... He just doesn't know how to jump the tree." Jesse wasn't the horse rider the girls were.

From far off in the darkness, on the other side of the fallen tree, came a yell. "But I have a *driver's license!*"

The three girls took their time to find a way around the destruction and get Jesse out. With the danger passed, they all felt their bodies go limp, as well as go cold at the realization of how close they came to being sucked into the air.

"We need to stop and rest," Bess said. "We can follow that thing better when we can think."

Darkness started to engulf the teens. The space ship was now far away and tearing through the land to the south. Even if it got near to her father, they would see and hear it well before it got to them. Bess hoped so, at least.

"Let's stop for the rest of the night," Aurora yawned and shivered from the exhaustion and stress. "We'll be no good for anything, and our poor horses are terrified. They probably won't sleep at all tonight."

Bess and the rest agreed. They had barely fallen asleep before the space ship had come to Earth, and now they were only more tired. Things were worse. Much worse. But not sleeping through the night wouldn't make things better.

This time, the four of them simply tied the horses to allow them to graze, then they all went to sleep on bedrolls. No fire, no food. Their bodies needed no encouragement to fall asleep.

They would sleep like the dead through the night. No one would wake until the sun had already started to color the sky. The mountains to the east cast long shadows into the west. The teens slept into the cool morning when the sky turned quickly from purple to a mix of orange and blue.

Bess woke to the sound of someone singing.

She got up, rubbed the sleep from her eyes, and tried to focus. Her feet hurt and her mouth was dry. Her back ached from riding so long. A good night's sleep was what she needed, but all she got was a night's sleep. Then she awoke to singing. Bess was sure she was hearing things.

She looked around and found where it was coming from.

Aurora stood in the field with the four horses, singing to them. Her horse, the beautiful and fast paint pony, walked up and nuzzled her. Bess walked over, barefoot, to see what she was doing.

"Since she was asleep," Aurora said, as horses generally slept standing up, "I sing to her from far away in the morning so I don't walk up and startle her. It's better than any alarm clock." Bess agreed. Aurora's voice was beautiful, especially when she sang her family's songs in her native language.

The rest of them arose and began to fix breakfast, then saddle the horses for the morning ride. Bess was able to take time to use her compass, along with basic marks she had on her handkerchief, to plot where they should go next.

"We should head back to where the Starlighter is," she said. "If they go to where the signal first came from, that's where they will be. I want to make sure they haven't found the Starlighter and the ship the refugees came on."

"Do you think we should get that close?" Jesse asked. "Shouldn't we go find your father first?"

"If those outlaws are there, we need to know. And my father won't be there. He planned from the beginning to be gone. He wouldn't stick around to let himself be captured."

They rode slowly, carefully avoiding the destruction made by the big flying saucer as it had scoured the ground of life in its wake.

It took about three hours, but the teens finally arrived at their first destination, near where the Starlighter and the old moon ship were hidden. Bess didn't want to get close, but she wanted to see if the ships had been discovered. From over a mile away, they found a place to shelter the horses while they spied with Bess's binoculars.

"Yeah, sure enough, they're there," Bess said. She found the big saucer landed on the bottom of the ridge, just below the hidden alcove where the two other ships were tucked. "But it doesn't look like they found the Starlighter yet. That's a good thing." The moon men seemed to be milling around under the saucer. With the location found, but no transponder there, they didn't know where to look.

Jesse took the binoculars from Bess. "Where is the Starlighter?" he asked.

"Just above them, hidden by a bunch of brush, in a cave."

"I can't even see where you mean," Jesse scanned the hillside. "Maybe there…" he saw a larger dark mass of mesquite and branches, "but if it's that well hidden, they may not even think to look up."

Aurora was looking, trying to see that far with her eyes. "What would they do?" she said. "You have to think about what they would think. They wouldn't think to hide. These guys probably just think the others are around somewhere, just waiting to be found. I would think they would have gone to hide in the trees, not in a cave. Maybe these fellahs don't know what cliffs are, huh?"

Bess hadn't considered that. She didn't like the idea of "think like a moon man", but Aurora was right. They would be figuring out things from their point of view. Which meant they would be making different choices than she would.

"Okay, at least they are stopped. Let's get going while they are all there. We are going the long way," she pointed out a path around the far end of a large forest of trees. "I don't want them to be able to look down and see us moving. We'll hide in this edge of the forest as we go south, then around to this point."

She touched a spot on her handkerchief. "That's point one of where my father said he would go."

"What about that one?" Lydia asked about a point even closer.

"I put that there in case I lost this," she waved the handkerchief. "I didn't want any marks that identified one place as more important than another. For all they know, that could just be a watering hole."

"Good thinkin'" Jesse said, though in his mind he didn't like to think about being captured by the moon men.

"Let's go, we're burning daylight," Bess insisted as she got up. She put her binoculars away and mounted her horse. The others followed quickly.

A long ride of more hours meant that they were being cautious, but also it meant more time until they met back up with Bess's father. It seemed to take all day, but Bess and her friends kept each other safe, talking about other things. They discussed swimming in Bess's pool, new clothes, new music. Any subject was good enough to keep the worries out of their mind. It allowed the long trip to go by a little faster for the four friends.

Bess finally got to the rendezvous point where she was supposed to meet her father. It wasn't a specific place, but more of an area that allowed access to water and some form of shelter. In this case, it was a large and thick wedge of oak trees that towered over leaning brush and green grass that grew up near a stream bank. There was no trace of her father or the others.

"There has to be some sign of them," encouraged Aurora.

"Did they plan to leave a marker or something?" asked Lydia, who looked around for any marker of human life. The whole place looked undisturbed.

"No," Bess answered. She had left so fast, they made no detailed plans other than a vague area to meet. She thought for a moment about who she was looking for. Her father, yes, but also families, older people, groups that were scared and wanted to hide.

"Lydia, where would you go?"

Lydia looked around. There was a copse of trees, taller than the others, that seemed to be hidden by low growing brush around the outside. The stream meandered into the area in a wide curve. It was like an arroyo, only narrower and probably a bit deeper. The water looked cool, trickling. It would be the place Lydia thought she would go to soak her tired feet if she were here. Which she was.

"In there," she said, confidently.

The four clucked at their rides and sloshed into the stream. They followed it into the meander as it turned slowly into the big grove ahead. There still was no sign of anyone at first. Bess kept scouring the tall trees, even looking up to see if they had jumped into the branches. That's what she would have done.

Lydia was looking somewhere else. She was looking down. Then she saw what she was looking for.

A pair of green eyes stared out from beneath a thick dark green mass of leaves.

# CHAPTER 16

## A Better Chance At Freedom

"Children!"

Lydia called out to her friends. "Look, here, we found them!

"It's alright, we're friends, you can come out." Lydia dismounted her horse, but didn't go anywhere near the bush hiding the eyes. Nothing moved, but she saw more eyes appear. Kids were curious, she knew, and they would have to see what's going on.

Finally, one, a young girl, came out of the brush. She looked from Lydia to her horse and back. She seemed fascinated both with Lydia's curly blonde hair and the large, snorting beast on which she rode.

"It's okay," she said, "You can pet her. She likes kids." Lydia went over and stroke her horse's mane.

Now, more people came out. Bess counted about fifty of them. They looked mostly like families, with a few older people as well, maybe grandparents.

Bess got off her horse and asked, "Where is my father? Is he here?"

"Are you Bess? Bess Truly?" one of the older women spoke up. "We didn't expect four of you."

"Neither did I," Bess laughed. The others didn't know what was so funny. "These are my friends. They came out to help me the day after I left. Now, where is my father?"

"He went with some of us to find another place to hide. He said he was going to find a path out. He said he would be back soon if he found something. We were supposed to stay hidden if anyone showed up except for you."

Bess thought that made sense. They didn't know her. Only a few of them had seen her, and those people were probably all with her father.

"Let's get the horses brushed and start some," she looked at her watch; they had been riding all morning. "Lunch?" It was almost a guess. They just needed some food in them.

Aurora looked at the kids. "I bet they could use a bite, too."

Jesse weighed the canned food he had in his bags. "We probably don't have enough for everyone. We will just have to share what we do have. I bet the kids would like some peaches and pears." He waved two cans at his friends.

So the four teens did what they could to share their rations with the families and children. The kids were incredibly interested in the sweet fruits. Jesse felt bad that he had to cut the fruit into tiny slices so that they all got a taste. Lydia made a watery punch with the juice from the cans.

Bess was happy to see the families were safe, but she really wanted to find out where her father was. She had only just found him, and now he was gone again. Bess was at the point of just marching them all out of the valley, through the mountains, and to the nearest town. "Put them on a bus to Three Winds," just like she had thought of the day before.

The moon men in their giant saucer complicated things, but at least they didn't know where the refugees were.

It would be a long three hours until until some of the first jump pack laden refugees returned. The children and family members were visibly relieved to have them back. "Are they all extended families?" Aurora asked. Bess had no idea.

"I would guess they are families in one way, at least," she said. "Kind of like us. Things just seem better when we are together. We may not look alike, you and me, but still..." Bess nodded out at the members of the group reuniting.

She was right. Bess with her wild waving strawberry blonde hair, tall and skinny, looked nothing like Aurora's straight raven black hair that hung long over her back. And neither looked like Lydia, with her tight ringlets that she would always try to manage, until they got into situations like this and it blew into wild tumbles that she tugged at to tame.

And none of them looked anything like Jesse, with his rosy pink face and short sandy hair. They weren't related; they didn't come from remotely similar places, but they were close like family. They looked out for each other and valued each other preciously. Their friendship was more valuable than gold.

"I bet they feel the same way about each other that we do. Family or not."

Thinking about family, Bess looked as the last of the jump packs came bounding in through the trees. She recognized her father immediately as he came in for a heavy landing.

"Oof! I felt that one!" Steve Truly tried to hide the heavy impact with a smile, but he was still recovering from a broken arm. It must have hurt more than he let on when he landed. "I'm still not used to this thing!"

Jesse came running up quickly. He and the other Zap-Gun Rangers hadn't seen the jump packs yet, and he was properly amazed.

"Hey, kiddo! I see you called in the cavalry," he said as he looked around at the two new girls and one new boy in the midst. "How'd your trip go, okay? Is this the only run-in you had?"

Bess filled him in on the saucer and their near miss escape. All the while, Jesse kept looking at the strange backpacks that some of the refugees wore. "In due time, Jesse. I don't blame you wanting to try these out. But this isn't the time or place," Steve explained. "We found a cabin about six hours walk from here, faster with these things. It's a good shelter spot, and only two hours to a trailhead on the other side of the mountains. If that saucer starts looking, we need to be far away as soon as we can."

Bess and Lydia began the work of gathering up the rest of the kids, while Steve showed Aurora, Jesse, and the other members of the group just where they were going to go. It was an old cabin built 25 years earlier for a geologist to work and live. It would have some food, but mostly it had walls and roof. It would be real shelter, and it had a real path out to the rest of the world. They could spend the night and get away the next morning. "Jesse, I think you and one of the other Zap-Gun Rangers could go ahead on horses tomorrow and round up a bus or truck. If you get in early, you can call the agents for them to bring in help quickly. We'll need food, clothes, medicine, and definitely let them know the moon men are out here in the wild. I don't want to tangle with them again."

With that plan, the entire group began its move. Children were gathered and they began a slow walk toward the protection and shelter they needed.

Tomorrow, hopefully, they would get a better chance at freedom from their pursuers.

Bess, Aurora, and Lydia rode a rear guard, mostly to help pick up stragglers and tired walkers in case they slowed too much, but also to keep an eye out for anyone who might discover them. They weren't much, but they were better than nothing.

The first hour was slow going, but the trees offered shelter and hiding places. As soon as they broke through the woods, they were out in the open. It was mid afternoon, and the sun was still high. It would be easy to spot them, Bess thought.

It would also be easy to spot that big flying saucer, she thought, too.

She thought that because the first time she got a clear view of the mountains to her back, she saw it, far away, rising into the air.

Then it spun up, with its green glow visible even in daylight, and began to head in their direction.

# CHAPTER 17

## Head'em Off At The Pass!

Up ahead, her father and the rest of the *brujas* and *brujos*, these wild rocket people on their jump packs, leapt into the air, leading the others onward. They didn't see the saucer, since they were so committed to leading people ahead. They didn't look back. It would only take one of them in the air for the saucer to see them and chase them down.

Bess could only hope that her father saw the saucer first, before they were noticed.

She saw twenty five of the jumpers leap into the air in a long line. "No way they don't get noticed," she said to Aurora and Lydia. "Alright, Lydia, no wait, Aurora," she had a plan in her head that changed with every beat of her fast pounding heart, "ride ahead and catch up with them, warn my father that the saucer has seen them, and to get moving, or hide. Lydia," she turned to her other friend, "we're going to gather up the kids here, even if we do it one

117

at a time, and ride them ahead. They are going to Be the most scared and slowest. We're going to leapfrog them ahead of the main group."

"Got it," Lydia said, and went to work without another word. She rode up to the last of the families, and had the first little girl scooped up into her arms. Then she took off in a cloud of dust. "No use trying to hide now," Bess said.

"We'll take the kids ahead," Bess yelled to the few parents and grandparents, the older members of the group, "we can go faster than on foot!"

Bess was handed another child that she took into her saddle, and with a shake of the reins and a prompting kick, she called out, "Go, Electra!"
The horse sensed both the added weight, and the added need to move. Well rested from a long night's sleep and three hours of happily grazing, Electra was in rare form. In front of her, Bess could see Lydia on her horse. Bess was gaining on her.

They got to the front of the main group and each dropped a kid off. Bess didn't see Aurora or Jesse. "They must be farther ahead," she hoped. Looking back, she saw the saucer plainly. It was definitely moving their way. But it seemed to be moving slower than before. Bess didn't know why, but she counted it as a small blessing as the refugees started to run faster.

She wasn't sure if it would help. They still had hours to go, and little cover. That saucer and its evil outlaw moon men inside could close the distance in minutes if they wanted to. Even if they didn't, the refugees were discovered.

Bess rode quickly to the back of the line to pick up another child.

She was able to get six kids, as well as Lydia carrying six more, before she met with her father, who landed back into the large group of people. "We can't outrun them," he said, "and we're about out of places to hide." He looked over the barren mountains and the nearly hidden trail that climbed and switched back and forth through a narrow pass. They still had over four hours to go.

"Can you take anyone with those things?" Bess asked.

"Yes, but not as far for every hop," Steve was sweating now, and wincing in some pain. But he was still a tough Texas cowboy, and wasn't going to go down without a fight. "Listen, we can take the kids, the lighter adults, and move faster. The twenty five of us will each take a child and if we can, one of the parents, and jump up the path. If we can cut the corners, instead of walking, we can make it all the way to the cabin in an hour, maybe less." He looked out at the saucer, still far away, but moving inexorably closer. It dipped one side toward the treeline that it tried so hard to avoid. "Remember how they had problems with our gravity? I bet they are having problems. But they will get used to it quickly."

Bess remembered all the ground, rocks, and trees that got sucked up when the saucer passed over them. "It may have some damage that they haven't had time to fix. But we can't count on our luck. They must know where we are.

"I think you have a plan, Dad."

Steve and the rest of the flyers took the children and a couple of the smaller parents in their arms, and began to leap from ledge to ledge. They may only have gone twenty feet in the air, but they began to move quickly. Bess still wished she knew where Aurora and Jesse were. Aurora had warned her father, but had not come back. Jesse was way ahead of them to begin with. He may have continued up the trail to see if he could find help.

Bess rode back to the end of the group. "It's like pushing a herd," she thought, then realized that these were people, not cattle. It wasn't fair to them to think that way. "Still, I'm riding drag," she thought. The drag rider was at the back of the group, helping to push forward, and making sure no one got lost. In her case, Bess was the last, she and Lydia. Bess realized that meant that she and Lydia might be the first ones discovered by the moon men in their saucer. "I wish there was a way to lead them away," she said. "We may have to put up a fight."

Lydia rode quietly beside her. "We've done it before," she said seriously. Bess stared at her. Lydia always looked perfect, beautiful, all cleaned up. But when someone did her wrong, she was a fierce and scary sight. Bess remembered staring down the refugees when they all jumped down on the landing where the Starlighter was. She was ready to take them all on single handedly. Lydia had the same look on her face now.

Bess took in what Lydia just said, with silent grave concern. The saucer looked like it had started to counter the strange change in weight now that it was on Earth. It lifted higher as it stabilized in the air. There was no doubt that they had been seen by the saucer, all of them. Or some of them at least. The saucer wobbled as it flew, but now it flew straight. They would be only minutes away from the big space ship coming after them. With all the refugees out in the open, some still climbing the mountain path, and hours away from any shelter that she knew of, there was little that could stop the saucer.

"They will probably come up this way," Bess motioned down the hillside, at the long strand of woods from where they had just come. "That was our last bit of cover. If we ride back into those trees, we can hide from them. They won't see us."

Lydia looked at the rest of the group, still moving forward in the distance. "What about them?!"

she asked. She didn't think Bess was going to run and hide and abandon all those people.

"We're gonna buy my father, and Aurora and Jesse, and all of them some time," she answered. She patted her Zap-Gun. "You an' me, cowgirl, we're gonna head 'em off at the pass!"

# CHAPTER 18

## Turn Out The Lights

Bess and Lydia took off back down the hill. Two girls on horses compared to an entire group of escaping people on foot probably wouldn't be noticed as they went the other way. Bess knew how hard it was to make out detail from higher up. She hoped the moon men wouldn't notice them until they wanted to be noticed.

"We get into the woods, and then we're gonna light them up," she said. She held her reins instead of holding her Zap-Gun. She wouldn't need it yet, and she did need the speed to get to the trees.

"We may not do much good against that thing," Lydia almost shouted the words. The ship was getting closer by the second.

"We don't have to do much damage, just make them think that there is a danger out there. Either they will turn and run or come after us. Once we are in the trees," Bess stopped and huffed as Electra jumped a low stone, "we can run through cover. If we need to, we can separate. After all this, meet me at the trailhead back there, but only at dusk or later. I don't want them to see us, at all."

Bess and Lydia stormed into the woods, looking for cover while still letting them see the sky. They found a small glade that let them look up over the mountainside and sky, but the trees around gave them some protection. "I wish it was darker," Bess said. They still had hours to go before sunset and twilight.

"I'll turn out their lights right now," Lydia growled.

"Just remember, just enough to get their attention, then run. Don't let them find you."

The saucer was close now. Bess and Lydia could feel the ground tremble from the pressure of the gravity waves the ship made. It appeared at the base of the mountain. To Bess it looked as if it was facing straight at the poor people who were climbing the path and trying to escape the ship, somehow.

Bess drew her Zap-Gun, and dialed the power setting up to high, with a distinctive *click*. Lydia did the same. Bess wished she had Aurora with them. Three would be better than two, she thought. But three might be easier to find. "Alright, three, two, one," her voice cracked with strain and worry, "punch'em!"

Twin blue flames of light, straight and crackling with power, emitted from the two Zap-Guns. They hardly had to aim at such a big target, even from far away. At about a hundred feet the bolts struck, tearing at the ugly green paint. The skin of the ship started to flake and peel.

"Again, aim for something important," Bess could only guess at what was important on the ship. She hoped to pop open a window or a hatch. Better yet, tear up one of the engine ducts to slow the ship or bring it down.

Bess leveled her Zap-Gun for another long blast. This time she raked the blue beam across the ship's hull. Some small nacelle with a grate was in the way. She pushed the beam across it, and was rewarded with a piece of metal falling off.

On the other side of the clearing, Lydia had good fortune as well. She found what was a door or access. It shook and twisted in the heat of the blue beam. Strange static coursed across the metal, then sparks, then more sparks, and finally the door popped with a muffled bang. It wasn't anything to stop the ship, but they would notice an open door.

"Let's move," Bess yelled. She took off into the woods in one direction, Lydia in another. The space ship had stopped, as if it was looking at who was shooting at it with a slingshot. The blasts from the Zap-Guns had been ferocious, but had done little real damage. They weren't meant for that type of destruction.

Bess stopped and wheeled Electra around to aim and fire again. Already, she saw Lydia pouring out blue electricity into the ship. She aimed at whatever would make a good target. One shot tore across the entire edge of the ship. Paint peeled off in huge flakes, and the metal underneath was exposed as a dull gleaming silver.

Bess was father away, which meant the ship was closer to horizontal to her. She could see some of the top now, instead of being stuck near the underside. Bess lit up her Zap-Gun with an aimed shot at the top. There were lots of windows up there, along with a round domed canopy. Bess worried it had one of their horrendous atomic weapons that could cut holes into the mountains if they chose to. It remained closed so far.

Bess's blue line scraped over the upper deck of the ship. The blue beam started straight and powerful, but as soon as it hit the top of the ship, it scattered as it made contact with all kinds of things on the upper deck. Antennas, bolts, hand holds, she didn't care.

But it turned out the moon men did care. They cared a lot. The ship rotated and turned toward them. Now the moon men knew there was a real threat, and they had to answer it.

Bess put her Zap-Gun in her holster and took off. She hoped Lydia was doing the same. If they just ran, and didn't fire, the moon men would hopefully keep looking. "And never find us," Bess wished.

She rode as quickly as she could through the woods. Keeping Electra under the cover of the leaves gave her a sense of security. For all she knew, the moon men may be following her with spooky eye sights that could see through the trees. It made her shiver with the thought. "So it's better that I don't think about it," she told herself.

Lydia lit up the sky with another blast at the ship. With the two of them, the moon men didn't know who to follow, if they could even find them.

The hiding spots and attacks from the forest were definitely bothering the moon men. Bess watched as the ship came down closer to the forest. The big gravity engines began to pull away at the trees near where Lydia had been.

"That's the plan," Bess thought. "If they can't see us, they will just remove the forest." It was a horribly simple plan, but it was one that would work. "I hope Lydia gets out of the way."

Bess rode as far as she could away and to the side of the big ship. She needed to be away from it before she lit her Zap-Gun again. Bess wanted the ship to come after her, not Lydia. Bess knew that Lydia was probably thinking the same thing.

Just as the ship settled down to rip up at the treeline, Bess aimed carefully at the tail of the ship. It was only the tail in that the front seemed to have the big clear dome on it, and this side had more of the exhaust outlets. She pulled her trigger and lit up the ship. From that far away, a lot of the power was wasted in the air around the beam. By the time it got to the ship, it was a sparkling haze that made the rear engines glow.

The moon men still didn't like that. The ship turned, and came after Bess, who again began to ride as quickly as she could away from the spot where she last was.

She was long gone from there when it got to the spot. That was when Lydia again lit into the ship from her far distant spot.

But this time the ship didn't turn. It kept going. It moved over and then away from the edge of the forest, back toward the landing place where it had been just an hour or so before.

Bess felt herself relax, then slump in the saddle. Another long struggle and ride with little time to rest had taken a lot of energy out of her. She got off of Electra to let her horse rest after a terrifying ride. Bess stared off into the distance to where the flying saucer had gone. It was already nearing the landing spot it had been at before, the same one Bess had found that was the best and only choice for a landing. She hadn't done much damage with her Zap-Gun, but she had made them run away to lick their wounds. They would be back soon. Hopefully there was enough time for everyone in the group to get away. They would need a few more hours to get the rest of the refugees through the mountain pass and to the cabin.

Bess looked around at the destruction caused by the big ship's gravity waves. Trees were uprooted or fallen over. "At least they didn't dig big holes in the ground this time," Bess thought. She realized just how long it would take for those trees to grow back. This was decades of damage in mere minutes. "How can they be so cruel?" she wondered aloud.

Bess didn't have time to worry. She got back on Electra so she could go look for Lydia. It was still light out, and Bess didn't think Lydia would go back to the trail this soon. Bess just wanted to be around someone else, for reassurance. She saw what one more person with her could do. She needed to find Lydia, and then find the rest of her friends.

It was another half hour before she found Lydia, who was walking in front of her horse. "Are you okay?!" Bess asked anxiously. "I was getting worried."

"Yeah," Lydia said, "me, too." She acted disappointed. "I was hoping we could have stopped them here." Lydia fumed at what she thought was a failure.

"We sent them back, and kept them away from those families, at least for now. We only need another hour or two. Let's get back to the trail head. Maybe we can see how far they got while we did our distraction."
Lydia got on her horse, but was clearly not happy

with the result. Bess tried to ease her mind on the ride, saying they had accomplished what they planned. "Hopefully, Dad got all the kids safe, at least."

They made their way slowly toward the mountain and the trail that led up it. "We should be able to catch up with them quickly," Bess said. "Our horses will make much better time than a group on foot."

But when Bess and Lydia got to the trailhead, they discovered that about half the group was waiting for them, hiding in the rocks and low brush. They never made it up the mountain.

"Why are you still here?!" Bess asked. She couldn't believe they would come back down from the trail. There were still about thirty of them, gathered together.

"When the saucer came, he had nowhere to hide," explained one of them. "We came back down because we didn't want to get trapped on the mountain."

Bess was upset, but to be fair, she and Lydia had done almost the same thing. "I should have told you want we were doing," she said to them. "I don't blame you, That ship is pretty scary.

"We need to wait until it gets a little darker, then you can begin moving up the trail. At least we are closer than before. Going at night will be difficult, but this is at least a real path. You can find your way. We need to get you back with the rest of them, with the kids up at the cabin. At least the saucer is farther off now." It was little comfort. The space ship could cover the ground in an instant if they wanted to.

Bess looked back over to where the saucer had landed. It was far away, and below the rocky outline of the edge of the mountains, masked by the trees.

Just then, her worst fears came back to her. The saucer started to rise. It went higher, and higher. No longer was it going to hover over the land, risking attack from Bess and her Zap-Gun.

"Oh, no," Bess said, "they are going for the cabin."

# CHAPTER 19

## Darker Downhill

There was no time to think. Bess had to act. She and Lydia leaned into the saddles of their horses. There was no time.

Bess watched the ship sail up and over the mountain far to the north of her. It was so easy for the saucer. It had to follow no trail or path, it didn't get hot or tired or feel pain. It just lifted up and went.

"How do you know they are going toward the cabin?" Lydia yelled as she bounced in the saddle.

"I don't," Bess answered, "but if they are going that way, they either know that's where my father went, or they will see it soon enough. We're never going to make it in time."

Even if they did, Bess didn't know what she would do next. There was no way to face off against who knew how many moon men armed with deadly atomic ray guns. If she had to, Bess was going to spit in their eye and heave rocks at them. She urged Electra onward.

The two horses and riders struggled and panted their way up the mountainside trail. It had a few narrow switchbacks, but was actually fairly straight, just with some steep elevation. They were surprised when they found an old white blaze marker on a wooden post at a narrow point in the trail. She stopped for a moment to look around.

"What are you looking for?" Lydia asked her friend.

"That." Bess pointed to a large flat area coming off the cliff side wall. There was a small circle in the stone. "It's a USGS Survey Marker. It tells us the height we are at."

"I can tell you that," Lydia stopped to take a drink from her canteen, then carried on, "we're high up, but not as high as that." She then nodded at the tall peaks on each side of her.

"No, this is a good thing," Bess explained. The United States Geological Survey placed markers all over the country to set specific height and location markers, even out in the wilderness, to help determine the heights of mountains and landmarks. This one had probably been placed over fifty years before. "It had to be placed here because this would be a high point in the trail. It means from here on, we at least are going down."

That news was welcome relief to the two girls, as well as the two horses. It also tamed some of the wild abandon in Bess. She just couldn't hurry herself, and Lydia, along. There were other people at stake here now. Bess suggested they walk their horses for a little bit.

"The sun is finally lower now, and we'll be in shade at least," she pointed out. "It will be harder to spot us on this side of the ridge. Bess looked up into the orange and blue sky. She didn't see the saucer in the air, which was an ominous sign. She knew it must have landed somewhere.

Once they cleared the small crevasse to the other side of the mountain range, the path began to meander, slowly, in a twisted and roundabout trail. It lead away from where Bess wanted to go. She and Lydia finally stopped to rest at a small spot with enough grass for their horses to eat. "I wonder how far behind the others are," Bess mentioned to Lydia.

"I just wish we could see where we are going," answered Lydia. The trees and rocks blocked any view of where the trail led.

Bess agreed. She would like to see where the saucer ended up. Her drawing on her handkerchief barely plotted where the cabin was. It didn't have anything like a trail marked on there. She didn't think she would need to have a map of the path. "We need to be careful," she said. "I don't want us surprised by those moon men if we stumble on them."

The rest of the way was painfully slow. The trail twisted back on itself many times. They wondered if they would ever get close to the cabin, they went so slowly. Bess was right about one thing, though. With the sun setting and the approaching darkness, it would be hard for anyone to see them.

It also meant that it was getting harder to see.

"We have to be getting closer now," Bess told Lydia. The trail had finally opened up. They had less than a mile to where the cabin stood. The path would be relatively straight, flat, and wide.

Electra snorted and slowed her gait. "Hold on," Bess whispered. She and Lydia pulled the reins to stop their horses. She climbed off Electra and handed the reins to Lydia. If Electra was getting nervous, Bess knew she should be, too.

It was darker still, but there was enough light to see well through her binoculars. Bess rounded a turn, where a wide copse of trees stood that flowed out into an open plain as random eccentric scars into a sandy land. Bess propped up on a low boulder to look over the area.

He found the cabin quickly. It was a low stone building that looked strong and fortified. It would be a great place to let the kids have real shelter after being out in the wilderness for so long. Bess could see a light on in the cabin. Then she saw someone move around outside. From afar, it was first difficult to make out who it was. It didn't look like anyone who had been with her father.

It was a tall figure, dressed in black, a long thick cloak and tight headpiece around his skull. Bess recognized the particular costume of the invading moon men immediately. These weren't kids and parents. The moon men had found them.

Bess could see, partly hidden in a grove of maple trees, the saucer, nestled into the woods.

The moon men had taken the children hostage, Bess realized. The danger had only grown. She wondered if her father was inside, or Aurora and Jesse. Where were they?

Suddenly, she saw a blue light reflect off the boulder on which she leaned. The bright beam would easily give away their location.

Bess turned back to stop Lydia when she saw why Lydia had her Zap-Gun out. Several dark shapes had moved out of the underbrush toward them.

# CHAPTER 20

## The Cabin Raid

"Put the light out!" whispered a scared voice.

Lydia turned off her Zap-Gun as Bess ran toward the figures. They hadn't moved any closer to Lydia, but Bess couldn't be sure who they were yet. She could charge in and confront the people, or try to sneak around and find out who they were. She knew in a heartbeat what she wanted to do. She was tired of sneaking.

"Who are you? Come out!" she said in a low growling voice. Bess had her Zap-Gun out, but not on. She didn't want any light shining towards the cabin in case it would alert the moon men there that she was close.

"It's us," said a woman's voice. Bess looked toward the person speaking. It was one of the women who wore those jump packs. Her father must be near. "They just showed up. We all tried to get away, but there was nowhere to go. They surrounded the cabin.

Only half of us could hide. They," she began to choke up, "they have our children."

Bess put away her Zap-Gun and moved toward the woman. Lydia got down from her horse, and came over as well. Bess hugged her. It felt small and useless, but she knew the mother needed support. "We'll get them back. They won't get away.

"Where's my father?" she asked, looking around.

"We think he's just ahead," said another man. "When we jumped, we went in two directions. We have been moving back this way, hoping to find them. We haven't been moving fast. It's getting dark and we can't see as well now. We're just trying to hide, and figure out what to do."

"I need to find my father," Bess said. "He'll know what to do."

Five minutes later, after Bess had walked silently through the overgrown brush near the trail, Bess had found Steve Truly and got filled in on what happened. "We saw the saucer coming over the mountain, but we didn't know if they had found us until it landed nearby. Half of us," he pointed to the other jumpsuited refugees, "had already taken off our packs. They came storming out of the ship before we could gather up the kids." He shook his head in dismay. "I don't know what to do."

Those were words Bess didn't want to hear. "We need to save those kids and the parents," she insisted, even though she, too, had no idea how to do that. "Where are Aurora and Jesse?" In all the excitement, she had forgotten that her two friends had ridden ahead of Lydia and her.

"I sent them on ahead," Steve explained. "I wanted Jesse to get as close to civilization as possible. Hopefully he made it and can call for help, but I don't know. It's getting so dark."

"Yeah..." Bess replied. "It *is* getting dark."

That gave Bess the seed of a plan.

"Look, we know they can't see well in the dark. Those moon goons are used to bright lights, and need light to see things coming. They can't see that far into the darkness, and it's going to get real dark real fast." She stared out at the far off cabin. She could now see the saucer, about a half a mile away. She pulled out her binoculars to spy it. "Yeah, look, most of them are just loitering around the saucer. It's the only thing that is making light out here." She looked over at the cabin. She could see the difference with only a few oil lamps burning in the windows. It looked like there were only a few guards out in the dark.

Steve took the binoculars and looked at what Bess described. "You're right," he said. "We need to move on this before they get organized.

"But we need to think about what happens after that. We may be able to get them out of that cabin, but there's no way we can all make it down the trail in the dark, find a place and a vehicle for all these people. We need a bus."

"A bus, huh?" Bess had an idea, but it would have to wait. First things first. They needed a plan to save those people trapped in the cabin.

An hour later, they had one.

Bess and her father stood no more than one hundred feet away from the house. Hidden in darkness, they had walked as slowly as possible to get to a spot where they could hide but see into the cabin. Steve counted no more than five of the moon men around the house. He could see inside, but there was little movement in there. Occasionally, a small face would look out the window. "They are keeping them all inside," he said.

"That's probably a good thing," Bess whispered back. "I don't like you going there without me."

"It's just too far, and we need you here. I don't want to put you in any more danger than I have to, kiddo. These folks, they have a stake in this. They want to be in the fight. They have been running, Now we have to let them lead."

It was too far, Bess knew that. It was too far to cover that open ground between where she was and where the cabin was, even in the darkness. The moon men that stood guard may be armed with their strange weapons, small atomic pistols that made gigantic explosions. It was dangerous.

Steve's plan was for his group of flyers to spring over to the cabin, all at once. They would take the few guards by surprise, hopefully, and then free the people in the cabin. It was Bess's job to guide them to her, and then they had to hide in the darkness. Hopefully before the rest of the moon men over at the saucer discovered what was happening and came running.

After that came Bess's idea. She just needed her father with her.

"Well, no use waitin' around for the cavalry," Steve joked. He looked behind him. There, hidden in the dark, behind the few bushes and trees around the cabin, were the twelve others that had escaped when the moon men had taken the cabin. Bess could barely see them, they stood so still. She imagined what their faces looked like. She knew they were mostly women, mothers of children. She remembered how she felt when she discovered her father was missing. This had to feel much, much worse. Her father was right, this was their time, and pity to poor moon goon that stood in their way.

Steve stood up, ran four steps, and jumped silently into the star filled sky. Twelve *bruja* and *brujo* jumped right behind him. They looked terrifying. Thirteen black shapes that all just sprang up out of the ground without a sound and took off into the night. Bess shivered even though it was warm. If the moon men could see what was coming, they would be quaking in their boots, she thought.

It took only a few seconds for the attack to begin. Steve and his flyers landed on the roof with a soft touch that Bess couldn't even hear it from where she was. The moon men saw them and heard them, but only for an instant. Four of the flyers almost immediately jumped off the roof and aimed for the terrified guards. The black cloaked figures could do almost nothing to stop them. The flyers kicked out with their boots at the moon men. The repellers on their boots would normally push back to soften any landing, but this time they met a more giving subject, the bodies of the guards.

As the first two flyers jumped down at the guard by the door, they stuck their boots out. The push from the repellers slammed into the guard, who was knocked twenty feet away. He went flying into the darkness as he skidded out into the sand and rocks.

Another guard met a similar fate, only he went rolling away as he tumbled from a well placed kick as well. The two guards at the front door were certainly down, and probably out.

Steve tried to jump down to the door, but one of his flyers had already gotten there. She took her helmet off as she pushed the door open with a bang. Bess could hear her yell even from where she was.

"Everyone, out now! We have to go! Run to the woods!"

Steve landed behind her, and added, "Go to the blue light. Run and don't stop."

They needed no more words. The crowd of children and adults, some carrying the smaller kids, ran out the door.

Immediately, Bess knew, this was her sign. She pulled her Zap-Gun out and set it to a bright blue light, then held it in the air. Behind her, another fifty feet away, at the beginning of the trail back over the mountain, Lydia lit hers up, too.

There was shouting from over at the cabin. Bess kept her eyes on her father as best as she could. In seconds the cabin was empty, but they still had to cover the ground to her and then to Lydia in order to hide in the darkness and cover.

"Come on, come here, keep running!" Bess yelled at the people escaping. There was no reason to be quiet now. She wanted everyone to know where she was.

It took only moments for the cabin to empty. All the people inside knew to run away from the danger. There still was danger, however.

Steve first looked in the cabin, to make sure it was empty. He yelled out, "Anyone else in here? We need to go now!" Then he slammed the door shut behind him.

Two guards on the back of the cabin had been knocked down, but not out. Steve circled around the side of the cabin to make sure all of his flyers were safe and getting away. When he rounded the corner, he ran straight into a fifth guard.

Both were surprised by the other. The moon man tried first to grab at Steve, then struggled with his robe to pull out a weapon. Steve pushed the man, then stepped forward and hit him across the jaw with a fast right fist.

Steve cringed in pain. His arm was still hurt from a break he had last month. Hitting a guy in the jaw didn't do his hand any good, either. But he was better off than the other guy.

The moon man crumpled in a heap. Steve thought about going through his robe to remove the weapon, a deadly explosive pistol, and throw it away into the darkness. But he didn't want to touch the guy. Time was of the essence, too.

Bess saw all this happening, but could do little to help. To be honest, she thought her father was doing pretty well on his own.

Then she saw two shapes moving from out in the darkness. Two more guards had been hiding in the nearby trees, unseen by all. They were running straight toward Steve, who was still holding his arm as he looked around. Bess was too far away to warn him. They would be on her father within seconds.

Suddenly, two more shapes burst out of the darkness. Now there were four of them!

# CHAPTER 21

## A Long Jump

Bess took one step toward the cabin. She had to help her father. Four of the strange moon men were coming after him. She had only just gotten him and the other hostages back. She wasn't going to give these moon men any leverage.

But as soon as she stepped forward, there was a tremendous explosion right behind the first two guards. A great blue flash burst out into the night. Near the guards, a small boulder shattered into fragments, sending stone bits zinging out in all directions. One guard immediately spun around, clutching himself where the rocks stung him across his body. The other flung his cloak around him. The stones had ripped it into holes, but had given him a small measure of protection. The moon men wore armor as part of their costume, including a tight skullcap helmet that protected their heads.

The helmet wasn't enough for what happened next. One of the two figures who appeared out of the woods chased down the remaining moon guard. He raised a large dark shape and brought it down with a crash on the moon man's head. Everyone within fifty feet heard a loud ringing *bonk*.

As Bess finally got to where her father was, one moon man was moaning in pain while the other lay unconscious in the ground. Her father was close to the other figures that had come out of nowhere to save him. With the light of the saucer backlighting them, Bess could only see in silhouette. When she finally came up to the three figures, she was able to recognize them easily.

Steve stood next to the figure that had clobbered the moon guard, talking with him and shaking him lightly at the shoulder. Jesse Armstrong stood tall, with his ever present folding shovel, now bent severely after making contact with the moon man's helmet. Behind him, Aurora stood, feet apart, her Zap-Gun pointed down but still out and ready to use. "The Zap-Gun Rangers to the rescue!" boasted Steve.

"C'mon, no time for questions," Bess insisted, "We gotta get moving!" She pointed at the saucer in the field behind the cabin. It was far enough away that the moon men hadn't gotten close to the cabin, but they now knew something had happened. They were pouring out of the ship and running toward the cabin, with their weapons in hand.

"Yeah," Jesse said, "let's beat feet!"

They were the last four to leave the cabin. It took them moments to get back to the path over the mountains and catch up with the rest of the refugees. In the darkness, they were as well hidden from the pursuing moon men as they could be. They stood in small groups, all far enough away from each other that they wouldn't get noticed together. Then they waited.

Fifteen tense and silent minutes later, Steve figured that they had lost their pursuers in the night. "I think we are safe," he whispered.

The darkness was a double edged sword for the hiding refugees. The moon men couldn't search in the dark, since they couldn't see well. But the refugees, tired and still scared, could see little better, and they had no benefit of light from the saucer. They had to stay in the darkness, where everything was hidden from them, only feet away.

"We'll get a rising moon in a little while. At least we will have some light," Steve said as he stared off to the east.

Bess was busy, trying to find out how Aurora and Jesse appeared out of nowhere to save her father. "Where did you two come from?!"

"Your dad sent me ahead," Jesse explained. "But he said Aurora should go with me. It was getting dark and she's better on horseback than me."

"That's true," Aurora said.

"Everybody is better on horseback than me," Jesse agreed. "Anyway, we saw the saucer come over the mountain, and turned around. By the time we got back near the cabin, those moon men had taken it over. We hid under a bush in a comfy place. And then those two guards came over and sat down on a rock right in front of us! We couldn't get away."

"We figured that sooner or later, you would mount a rescue and we would jump in when we had a chance," explained Aurora, "and we had our chance!"

"Now, you're two for two on saving us from moon men, Jesse!" Bess congratulated him.

"But I'm out another shovel," he sighed. The hard helmet had bent his folding shovel out of shape.

"We've gotten everyone free," Steve said, "but we still aren't safe. They have us trapped on this side of the mountain. We can't get past them, and we don't have any other direction to go. We need to get these people safe soon. We will start running out of food probably tomorrow, if not already."

"I've got an idea, " Bess interrupted. "We need two things. We need a way to get all these people away from here. And we need to stop them," she pointed out into the dark. "We," she pointed at her father, "need to go get the Starlighter and their space ship, the bus."

Steve said nothing. He took in the idea, even though it wasn't a plan. Yet. Bess probably had more to say, so he waited.

Bess didn't speak for a moment, to wait for anyone to disagree. Everyone was used to Bess coming up with an idea, and then they acted on it. So they all listened.

"When the moon comes up soon, you and I will have enough light to see, at least. We go back, get both ships. They have to be charged by now. You said they were about half charged when we were there. The power even came on in the bus. We don't need to go far, just get them both over the mountain. It's only a few more miles past here to a road.

"I'll fly the Starlighter, fly over their saucer to distract it. Maybe they will chase me, even. I can outrun that thing easy. That will give you time to land the bus and load everyone up. We just need to get away from here."

"It's an idea," Steve agreed. "There's only a couple problems." He listed his concerns. "One is that we still can't walk out of here. We'll have to leave the horses tied up."

Bess interjected, "Electra is fine where she is. We can come get her tomorrow when the rest of the cavalry arrives. Once the moon men lose their prizes, they won't have much fight in them. I betcha the G-

Men are waiting to send in some help." What she said was true. The horses all had access to grass and water for a day. The wilderness supported all kinds of wildlife around them.

"And here's the other thing, the hard part," Steve said. "We can't get back to the ships quickly. It will take hours to walk back. And your horses are all whupped. They can't ride any farther. Heck," he rubbed his shoulder, "I'm not 100% myself. I'm up for it, don't get me wrong, kiddo," Steve said with a hidden smile, "but that's a long hike, hours away."

"We won't need hours, and we don't need to hike," Bess smiled back. "we can use those." She pointed to the backpacks Steve and his flying team wore. "Let me have one of those jump packs from your flying circus, and we can just jump down the mountain to them. The path is about ten miles, but as the crow flies, it's only a mile or so."

"You've never done this before," Steve said cautiously.

"Neither had you a couple days ago," Bess argued.

"She's got you there," Aurora almost laughed at the comment.

Steve glared at Bess's friend, but they were right. Bess was the only other person who could fly the Starlighter, and it took two hands to fly. The big space bus had been clunky and old, but it flew soft and slow, not twitchy and razor's edge sharp like the

Starlighter. They couldn't just wait until morning for the moon men to come out and find them.

As if in punctuation to Steve's thought, a bright flare popped up in the air, far off to the east. The moon men were looking already.

One of Steve's flyers was listening to the conversation. "There is something you can do with the repulsers," he said. "These power packs," pointing at the backpack with the long silver batteries, "can be stacked. If you put one on top of another, it gives you a lot more power. We never used it that way because we discovered we would go too high on the surface of the moon. But here in your gravity, it should almost double your height. You may be able to lift yourself forward well over 100 meters or more. And the landings will be slower and softer."

Steve liked the sound of that. His shoulder had taken a beating from being jarred on the landing, with the backpack pulling at him.

"That will let us move even faster," Bess said. "We can just follow the path back down the mountain. I can see that by moonlight, no problem. Then it's a quick couple of hops to the Starlighter."

"I wish you had some time and daylight to practice this," her father said gravely. "It's not hard to learn. It's pretty instinctive, but I still don't like just putting you up in the sky in the dark."

"She'll do fine," spoke up another flyer. She handed Bess her own helmet. "I had to learn on the fly, too. We aren't getting the choice of how we do things, are we? But you seem to be responding well. We all appreciate what you are doing for us. We won't forget this."

A bunch of the flyers had gathered around Bess, Steve, and the rest of her friends. Bess looked at all of them in the near dark. Even though the light was only just coming out from the low moon, she could see them well enough. When she had first seen them, they were all scared and worried. Now they all were serious, severe, and ready to act. They were counting on her. She wasn't going to let them down.

"Well, now's better than a minute later," she said. "Put this pack on me and show me how it works."

A short fifteen minutes later, Bess knew as much as anyone could know about the jump packs the other flyers had worn. Run, press the trigger, jump, keep your feet under you, aim with the heels for the landing. "Like Superman," Jesse said.

"Alright," Bess tightened the straps on her pack. It felt different than the loose backpack that had been bouncing around with stuff for days. She stared down the mountain side. She could see the trail she had come up earlier, glistening in the light of a moon and stars with the reflecting sand and bits of mica. "We need to move. Remember," she told her friends, "when we show up, be ready to go as soon as Dad lands with the bus. Anyone who can't make it, I'm counting on you to get them, and Electra, down the trail."

"We're set," said Lydia, who gave Bess a hug. "Go light the sky, Bess."

Bess turned, faced the direction she wanted, and with a nod to her father, the two put on their helmets. With a click, Bess flicked up the shield that darkened the eyepieces. Now the night sky was clear and crisp. She was ready.

One, two, three steps, Bess jumped into the air as she punched the little button attached to a cable. She felt herself go light. It was like jumping in the air, only she didn't come down. She had to resist the urge to yell with delight. Her body zoomed into the sky, high above the trail. She kept her head steady, looking forward, then spotting the place where she wanted to land. She felt a soft whir on her back, as some mysterious gyro kept her upright. She kept going up, up, up, then felt herself begin to fall.

It was a strange and awkward feeling. This was much higher than she had seen the flyers go. When they jumped, it almost looked believable, as if they had been sprung off a giant trampoline. She was truly flying, maybe 300 feet in the air. She couldn't see her father, who should be behind her. He had told her the one thing is to look where you are going. Don't look around. She knew he would be fine.

The only issue was that she had jumped much farther than she had thought she would. Bess passed over her landing spot while she was still going up. She quickly picked another place. It was a wide turn in the trail, near the bottom of the mountain. She leaned her feet out, like she was doing a long jump, and pointed her heels at the spot.

It was as if the jump pack knew where she had wanted to land. Bess felt herself glide down, like being on an invisible slide, that would end up right where she aimed. As she got close, she felt her heels get pushed back. It was almost as if a big cushion of air was forming under her. With the extra power of the jump packs, Bess almost floated down the last six feet. She landed like she stepped off a set of stairs.

A second later, her father landed next to her.

"Well," he said in his soft drawl, "That was a lot easier."

Bess pointed toward the northwest. "There's a spot there, can we make that jump?"

"I don't see why not," her father answered. This time, Steve ran forward, four steps, and jumped. Bess watched him for only a moment before she, too, ran forward and leapt into the sky.

The two figures were black shadows bounding into the darkness as they were lit by the stars and moon over the rugged prairie. It was no wonder people saw flying witches in the night here. It was a strange, unreal sight, to see people flying without wings or a plane.

Bess landed in front of her father a second after he touched down. "Let's just see how far up we can go," she suggested. "Those two open spots should be visible easily from up high. The white sand will be lit by the moonlight."

Steve agreed. "We have to be close, only a few more jumps. These extra batteries really make this easier." He flexed his knees to give the pack a little extra boost. Bess did the same.

Then the two took a step forward and leapt up, up, into the night sky.

It was incredible. They had to be up over five hundred feet, maybe more, Bess thought. It was almost frightening to be that high and think she would have to come back down, into the dark. But it was also exhilarating. She looked up at the sky, where the moon was now glowing like a bright lamp, and all the stars twinkled like pinpoint lights in the warm clear air.

As Bess was going up, she saw more light, too.

She was so high, she could see over the low, craggy mountains near her. To her right, she noticed a fuzzy glow that got brighter as she rose. Then she realized what it was.

The moon men had launched their saucer into the night sky.

Bess felt her jump reach its zenith, and she began to fall.

# CHAPTER 22

## Shaking In Their Boots

"We gotta move!" Bess proclaimed as she landed.

Her father had seen it, too. "We're close, but we have to be careful," he insisted. "We won't do any good with a broken ankle."

Or a broken neck, Bess said to herself.

"We are close," Steve insisted. "Maybe two more jumps. Look, kiddo," he put his hand out to her shoulder. "We land in that wide area beneath the ships, then jump up. I don't want to risk landing on that platform from far away. Those moon men aren't going to be able to find anyone very quickly. We need a minute to plan what we are going to do."

Bess agreed with her father. They first spotted a good landing point near some trees that was gleaming in the moonlight, an open meadow of grass. It was a quick and easy jump from where they were. They immediately ran, leapt into the air, and made it to the base of the cliff side where the two craft were hidden.

From there it was an easy jump up to the big plateau where Bess had first found her father almost two days before.

"Okay," Steve said as he began pulling off the coverings to the cave, "I'm going to get the Starlighter out, land it here, and you take over." Bess began to protest. She wanted to pilot the Starlighter. "No, it wasn't easy to do this in the daylight, and I don't want to risk you getting hurt or damaging the ships. We need both intact."

Bess knew he was right. Her father was a better pilot than her, and the Starlighter had been build for him originally, even if she had flown it several times. Flying out of a cave in the dark would definitely be difficult.

"After I get it out, you take over. You need to get going, do what you can to lead them away from the cabin and the path. Whatever you do, don't let them land near the cabin. We have to keep them in the air and away from the refugees. The one thing we can't have is that ship coming back to capture them again. Even if we can't get them on the bus," he jerked his thumb into the darkness at the big insectoid ship behind the Starlighter, "we have to make sure that saucer doesn't get near those people."

Bess only nodded. There was nothing else to say. Lydia, Aurora, and Jesse, along with all of the others, knew the plan. As soon as the saucer moved away, they all started moving down the path. It was about two miles from the cabin to a small house on the other side of the valley, and from there it was open dirt road. Jesse and Aurora would go ahead as fast as they could, make sure the path was clear, and call for help. If Bess and her father could keep the saucer from flying over the escaping refugees, they would be safe.

Lights came on in the Starlighter. Steve had disconnected the power lines and thrown them into the darkness. There was no time to be neat. Bess had no idea how he would lift the Starlighter into the air of the cave, then fly it out of that small opening. The Starlighter was meant to take off fast and high, not hover.

Bess stood outside the cave. She couldn't be near the silver craft when the hot electric sparks popped off under it. As soon as she was clear, she heard the familiar sound. A loud and fast *crackcrackcrack* echoed out. It sounded so different than from inside the cockpit. Inside, it was a regular humming thump, but from outside, it was a sharp electric popping sound. Bess almost expected the ship to burst through the cliffside.

But then it came out. It was covered in a blue-purple light, along with the white glow of landing lights to illuminate it. Her father had opened the fan ducts, which let much of the energy escape through the ring of the ship. The electricity coursed all around the Starlighter, giving it a menacing an ominous crackling glow.

Dust blew out of the cave, which only made the appearance more terrifying. "Those moon goons will be shaking in their boots when they see me coming," Bess thought.

Her father touched the ship down with a deft and soft kiss to the ground. The Starlighter almost immediately turned off. He jumped out of the cockpit hatch and left it open. "Your turn, kiddo," he smiled as he said it. "Go touch the sky, and show those moon men who's the sheriff here."

Bess climbed in and got settled. She saw her father run into the cave and begin climbing into the old moon shuttle. She waited only long enough to make sure he got in. With a wave, she lit the electric charge, and the Starlighter leapt off the ground and streaked into the night sky like a shooting star. The bright pulse of light under her lit up the mountainside. Bess made herself slow down, not hurry. She moved up and over the low mountain, then waited. Once in the air, the Starlighter could hover easily. She watched from out the side of her cockpit, as she waited for her father to emerge in the bus.

She didn't have to wait long.

The long ship came out less like the Starlighter, in its dramatic and menacing display. It was more like the mountain spit out a giant and ugly bug. The ship flew out, dust in its wake, gleaming and ugly green that Bess knew too well. It didn't seem to be able to hover like the Starlighter, but it definitely could move. Her father pushed the ship hard into a turn, then lifted it up higher and higher. As soon as Bess could tell that he would clear the cliff and make it over the mountain, she twisted the throttle on the Starlighter. It was time to light up the night.

The Starlighter lifted up high, well over the ridge line. She left the landing lights on. She not only didn't care if she was seen, she wanted to be. The bright lights, the hot popping electricity coming from underneath, along with the landing lights, were a promise to her friends that she was coming to help them. And a promise to the moon men in the orbiting saucer, which she could see easily from high above, that their time chasing people was at an end. She pushed the collective forward and sent the Starlighter hurdling toward the glowing saucer at high speed.

She wasn't even able to get up to the ship's top speed before she crossed paths with the moon men. Bess just flew right over them. She let the wake of the Starlighter buffet the saucer, sending it tumbling. It wobbled and tried to recover.

"That got their attention," she said, "now let's see if they want to play." Bess put the Starlighter into a hard turn, which pushed her deep into the pilot's seat. She tightened her muscles across her body, keeping herself tense. Then she quickly flattened out the ship. Bess looked behind her. The cockpit of the Starlighter afforded a clear view all around the circular ship, except for directly below her. She saw the saucer begin to rise and move toward her.

Bess began to circle the saucer from afar. The moon men tried to pursue her, but the big lumbering ship kept making a wider and wider arc, always chasing after where Bess had been, but not where she was. Bess realized if she kept circling, she would lead them back to where they were. She slammed the Starlighter into a hard braking move, then reversed course. She went higher and farther away from the cabin. In the darkness, the stars and moon were bright in how they lit the ground below. Bess could only barely see the light of the cabin and the little lamps that must have been in the windows. She knew she was going in the right direction. The saucer was following her, which meant they were going in the right direction, too.

Bess tried to keep her eyes on the saucer behind her, while flying forward, away from them. Her head was on a swivel as she looked back and forth. She was high enough that she shouldn't hit anything, she hoped, but she wasn't familiar with the land. She had to be careful.

Just then she saw the saucer begin to glow a brighter green. The ground below it first shone in a dirty haze, then cleared. It was lifting higher. Then she saw the bright green from above.

Bess threw the Starlighter into a fast dive, away from the mountains, while she poured electrical power to the ship. Her heart raced to keep up with the *thumpthumpthump* of the Starlighter. She tried to watch the saucer, but she lost it in a bright flash.

A streak of green energy coursed through the sky behind her, where she had just been. The moon men had decided they didn't just want to chase her. They wanted to shoot her out of the sky. "You have to do better than that," she said in the hollow quiet of the Starlighter.

As if on her command, another beam ripped across the sky, near enough that Bess imagined that she felt the crackle of energy from the beam. She couldn't tell if her scalp itched from the static or if it was just her imagination. She decided not to stick around to find out. She twisted the throttle, punched the Starlighter into the air, and took off away from the saucer at over 500 miles per hour.

Behind her, the saucer rose to give chase. It poured out power from its engines, punching a hole in the gravity of the Earth to make it rise and fly. Bess immediately dipped the Starlighter down, anticipating another shot. "These fellahs are faster on the mark than I thought. They're loaded for bear." But the sky stayed empty. Bess wasn't going to give them a target.

She was escaping at high speed. She wasn't too happy about it. She felt like she was abandoning her friends, but leading the saucer away was her job. She spun the Starlighter in the air so she could look far off into the distance to her right side.

She saw the big saucer still pursuing her, with the two domes on its top open and the big energy weapons out. Farther away, she could no longer see any detail from the cabin, but she could just make out the faint glow of the bus as her father began to maneuver the triangular ship toward a landing spot. It seemed to move so much more slowly than the saucer.

Just then, the moon men dipped their ship down and slowed it. They had seen the same thing Bess had. The big saucer began to lower toward the ground and spin. It may be big and fairly fast, but it couldn't turn like the Starlighter. Nothing could. It just happened to be much, much closer to the bus, and all the people on the ground.

They were going back for the refugees, Bess realized.

She saw the saucer, now low to the ground, as it burned through the soil, rocks, and plants that covered the summer prairie. All behind it, the saucer cut a path of destruction in its wake. "All that damage," Bess thought, "and all that could be done to those people on the ground." She hoped they had gotten away from there.

Then Bess realized they would all be running for the touchdown point, right where her father was landing.

# CHAPTER 23

## The Bus Stop

Her father must have seen the saucer, too. His big ship lumbered in a circle as he tried to gain altitude. He lifted up and away from the landing point near the cabin. The big triangular bus went higher and higher into the night sky.

Bess wasn't sure what she could do. If the moon men wouldn't chase her, she couldn't lead them away. They still were far away from where the refugees were, but they were getting closer by the moment.

Bess had no weapons on her ship. The Starlighter was not meant for that. She could possibly fly over them, hopefully to push the big saucer down. But the moon men had those horrible weapons that were much faster than she thought they would have been. Already she had been shot at with near misses. If she got closer, or if the saucer landed, they could easily aim at her as she flew overhead. She may not be a sitting duck, but a flying one was still possible to hit, she knew.

With that thought, the saucer erupted with a green glow from a blast of one of the big guns. A beam of atomic energy poured through the night sky directly at her. Bess felt the Starlighter fill with static electricity. Her hair stood up on end. The Starlighter rang with a high pitched whine where the bolt had ripped just off the side of the outer disc. It almost took a second for the air inside to heat up from the blast. Only after the energy beam had shot by her did Bess heave the Starlighter to the left as the beam passed over her right side.

The Starlighter still flew. She checked her gauges. She still had power, and the ship bobbed with her steering input. She jerked left then right. It was a good thing she did. Another blast from the other beam weapon poured energy in the direction of where she had been going. "They were trying to get me to go there!" Bess realized. The saucer had sent her into the path of the second shot. Only because of her quick reaction she wasn't hit by the powerful weapon's beam.

Bess twisted the power up on the collective and headed up and away. She was in too much of a risk. She headed east, then dipped down, hoping to throw off the targeting of the saucer. She would land if she had to, behind any low hill that would giver her protection. She felt bad that she had no way to stop the saucer.

She looked over her shoulder as she shook the Starlighter back and forth. The saucer was landing. It had made its way back toward the landing spot. Bess put the Starlighter into a curve. "Hopefully they used a lot of energy up and can't shoot at me right now," she wished. She had to see what the saucer was going to do. It was hovering at a couple hundred feet. She could see the gravity waves pouring from under it, holding the big ship up. Its landing legs began to extend on folding hinges. In moments, the ship would be able to unload the moon men who would chase down all the refugees.

Then Bess saw an amazing sight. Amazing, and horrifying.

Her father had turned the old moon ship he piloted from high above, and began to fly down toward the saucer. The two ships aimed for the same place, but only one was going to fit.

Then Bess realized what her father was going to do.

She twisted the control stick on the Starlighter, and threw the ship into a hard, tight turn. She felt the engine strain with the power, and the little winglets chattered in trying to hold the air back as she turned. Bess immediately went to full power, flying the Starlighter at over 500 miles per hour. She would get there in seconds.

It would be seconds too late.

She watched as the big bug eyed ship, piloted by her father, crashed into the glowing green saucer. At first it looked like the two would simply bounce off each other. Then the pointy nose of the bus wedged into the middle of the saucer. The weight of the old bus combined with the power from its engines slammed the saucer down. Bess watched as the saucer was pushed into the ground. The landing supports crumpled like tin. Then the entire ship flattened like a pancake onto the ground. Bits of green light energy burst from under the ship. Bess saw the light through a cloud of dust and rocks that were thrown out from the impact.

The old bus was impaled in the middle. It sat like a giant arrowhead, pinning the saucer to the ground. Bess kept her eyes on the ship, hoping against hope that it somehow stayed intact. She was terrified at what she might find.

Within seconds, she was over the wreckage of the two ships. She saw several of the moon men pouring out of the broken saucer. She couldn't land there. They would catch her and have the Starlighter for sure. She needed to land far enough away that they couldn't get to her. She needed her friends now, desperately.

Bess found a spot barely big enough to touch down. It was an agonizingly slow process as the Starlighter softly dropped down as it spiraled to the earth. Finally, with the electric power turned off, Bess jumped out of the hatch into the darkness.

Going from the lit cockpit of the Starlighter to the starry night of the Guadalupe Mountains made her nearly blind as she adjusted to the dark night. Finally, with the light of the moon glistening on the sand, casting black shadows behind every tree and bush, Bess was able to see.

It didn't help her much. There was nothing to see nearby. Only the glow of green energy behind the soft light of the cabin nearby, along with the occasional flame that spurted up from the crashed ships farther off lit up the land. Bess looked around, hoping to see someone, anyone. She tentatively began to take a step, then two, toward the crash. She had to get there to see if her father was there, if he was injured. But she hated to think of what she might find.

On her next step, she saw a soft blue light appear in the darkness to the east, near the treeline that marked the path that they were going to take to freedom and escape long ago. Someone was there, one of her Zap-Gun Rangers was sending her a signal.

Bess ran toward the light. Heedless to the danger of falling in the dark on the rough terrain, Bess sprinted toward her friends. She needed someone else to help her. If she had to fight her way through a wall of moon men to get to her father, she would need all the help she could get.

The light moved toward her. In moments, Bess was face to face with Lydia. The curly haired blonde girl looked tired and disheveled, with her hair in wild frizzy rings, and a twig stuck firmly behind her ear. But she smiled when she saw Bess. "Nice flying, Bess," she complimented her friend.

"Thanks," Bess said, breathless and excited, "but we need to get over there." She pointed toward the crash site. "I have to go find my father."

"Oh," Lydia smiled cryptically in the moonlight, with soft white teeth shining, "I don't think we need to worry about him."

Another figure stepped out of the darkness. "That was a good parking job you did, kiddo," as a long thin arm pointed out at the Starlighter, "but don't think we should leave it there."

# CHAPTER 24


## A Wake-Up Call


"I saw that saucer shooting at you," Steve explained, "and, well," he wiped his brow with an 'aw shucks' attitude, "I just couldn't let those outlaws get away with that."

"But how did you get out?!"

"I jumped," Steve patted the jump pack still on his back. "With this extra battery, it was pretty easy. I just popped open the hatch and jumped away. I wasn't going to let those outlaws get away with shooting at my girl, then landing and coming after all those folks. I knew I had to stop that saucer, permanently."

"But what about all the others? All those families?" Bess asked.

This time, Lydia spoke up. "They are already a mile down the path. They aren't anywhere near here. When we saw the saucer coming back, I sent them down the trail to meet up with Aurora and Jesse.

They are probably already at the old trailhead getting help.”

“Well, let’s get outta Dodge before those fellahs get organized. I gave’em a bloody nose, but they will have a chance once they clear the cobwebs.”

With that, Bess and  Lydia began the long walk away from the crash site. They led their horses in the darkness, with only the soft light of the moon to illuminate the path. In moments, overhead they saw the Starlighter fly off to the east. Bess watched it land nearby, likely at the trailhead. As they got closer, it took off again. Lydia wondered to Bess, “Where do you think he’s going?”

“I dunno,” answered Bess. “Probably going to an airport or a town. Maybe Carlsbad or White City. The Starlighter won’t have a lot of power left in it, but it will move faster than a horse.” Bess stopped and stretched her legs as she tried to rub her soles through her scuffed cowgirl boots. “Or our aching feet.”

“I agree,” Lydia said with a groan. “See, this is why I prefer tennis shoes.”

“You would feel every rock you stepped on,” Bess told her.

“But I could take them off and rub my toes,” Lydia responded. “And I’d look so cute!” She patted her wild hair.

“You always look cute,” Bess told her, “even when you are fighting off moon men!”

The fun banter made the hike pass by quickly. They arrived at the trailhead, which had a small cabin. It didn't provide much shelter, but it had some provisions and the notion of protection. It had two things that Bess greatly appreciated. It had a phone for emergencies, and her friend Aurora standing just outside. When Bess and Lydia appeared out of the darkness, she ran to them, hugging each tightly. "I'm so glad you're okay! That saucer shooting at you had us all scared to death!" Aurora pulled the twig out of Lydia's hair.

"How did that get there?" Lydia said. The other girls just laughed.

"Where's Jesse?" Bess asked, looking around.

"When we got here, he immediately started calling. He got to the G-Men, your pals, and told them what was going on. Then he woke up someone in Carlsbad, right before your father landed. The two of them took off together. Jesse said something about getting some buses here."

"I don't know if a bus can make it this far. But a truck probably could." Bess looked around in the darkness. "I think these folks have done enough walking. I just hope we can get them out of here quickly. We need to keep an eye out for those moon men. Though I think they have enough problems on their hands. Without a ship, they are stuck here, and they don't have any food or water. The fight is probably gone out of them. They just might want to show up out of spite, though."

So they waited. Exhaustion mixed with anxiety, and sleep won out, for a time. Bess curled up under a tree with her bedroll off of Electra, who seemed content to sleep standing up, blissfully unaware of all the events that happened around her.

An hour later, Bess was being nudged awake. She first was groggy, then a little mad. She was having such a wonderful dream, about being on a beach far away, with nothing but the gentle sounds of the ocean. It was so different from the dry warm night in the dry warm desert. "Whuh?!" she first stammered, then found her voice and remembered where she was. "What? Sorry, um, what's happening?"

One of the women from her father's flyers stood over her, softly shaking her awake. "Someone's coming," she said simply, pointing to the east.

Two sets of lights bounced up the twisting trail. Bess immediately knew these were regular vehicles, trucks of some kind. She didn't know who it was yet, whether the Army had found them or just some local park rangers saw weird lights in the sky and came to investigate. One thing was for sure, it wasn't a flying saucer from outer space. Bess almost considered going back to sleep and finishing that dream.

The two vehicles pulled up, bouncing away on the rough road. From the glare of the headlights, they could see a door open from a big truck with a covered back. Behind it came a pickup with a long trailer for horses. A voice spoke out in the dry desert air with a soft Texas twang, "Anyone need a lift?"

Steve Truly had shown up with a big old Ford deuce and a half truck that looked like it was from World War II, because it probably was. Behind him, Jesse hopped out of the pickup. The door creaked on its hinges as he slammed it shut. "How's this for a desert Cadillac?" he said. "We got a limousine for people," he pointed at the big truck, "and one for horses," as he jerked his thumb at the big carrier behind him.

It took a few trips, but they were able to slowly shuttle all the refugees down from the mountain to two waiting buses that Steve had somehow chartered in the middle of the night. "Yeah," he said with a wink, "You wake up somebody wanting a bus in the middle of the night, they are going to be cranky. You wake them up with a call from the FBI," he winked at the joke about the G-Men, "and they are ready to help serve their country."

It took all night, but by the next morning, all of the refugees had made it to Carlsbad, where they were treated to hearty meals. Steve took them all into stores and bought them new clothes as well. "You make it to Texas, and you don't even get a cowgirl hat?" he joked to one young girl, "Well, we can't have that."

Bess had fun helping the girls pick out hats, while the rest of the Zap-Gun Rangers showed off all the other clothes they could try on. Lydia in particular had a great time creating ensembles for the new arrivals. By the afternoon, they all looked like they were from the southwest. No one could distinguish them from anyone else except by their lack of an accent. "They will pick it up soon enough," Aurora said.

"I told you," Steve agreed. "I would just walk them out and put them on a bus.

"It just took a little while longer than I planned."

# CHAPTER 25

## Distant Neighbors

A week later, Bess sat by her pool back home at the C Bar M in Three Winds. It was the rare day that all three of her friends, with the addition of Jesse's girlfriend Annie, were all off from work and available to spend time together. Jesse would constantly jump off the diving board with a great splash as he cannonballed into the cool blue water.

"I think he's trying to empty the pool!" yelled Aurora over the noise.

"He's showing off for Annie," said Bess with a smile to the girl.

"He doesn't need to show off to me," she said back. "Watch this." And with a break in Jesse's relentless pattern, Annie slipped into the circle of a wet path from the pool ladder to the diving board. She walked up to it, stepped up, and with a graceful two steps and leap, she rose in the air, bent at the waist, and fell delicately into the water with her hands barely cutting the surface. Her body was straight up and down, with her toes the last to disappear into the deep end. She barely made a splash.

"Wow..." Lydia was impressed.

Jesse smiled wistfully. "Now who's showing off?"

"I am," said Annie.

"With a dive like that," Aurora said, still staring in awe, "you deserve to show off. Do that again!"

And with that, Anne began to teach the girls how to make a dive into the deep water of the pool. Jesse attempted it once or twice. He found himself tumbling over his head, rolling into a ball as he flipped over and over. "This is easier," he responded as he jumped off the board and grabbed his knees to his chest for yet another cannonball. The huge splash sent waves all over the girls.

"You're getting my towel all wet, Jesse," Lydia complained.

"Isn't that what it's supposed to do?" said Aurora.

Bess just laughed. Things were finally back to normal with her friends. Aurora and Lydia were teasing each other, Jesse was happily smiling at his wild mess he made. And Annie, well, Bess thought, maybe things were a little bit better than normal. She was glad to see Annie come out of her shy self now. She certainly seemed confidant, and she liked Jesse a lot. Annie didn't talk much, but Bess knew that's what Annie was like, and she was fine with it. As long as she was happy, and Jesse was, too, that's what she wanted.

A fun rock and roll song played on the radio that Jesse had brought with him to the pool. It was his local station, playing new music across the plains to entertain Bess and all the kids like her. The tinny sound was fine with her. It was an almost perfect day.

Her father showed up to make it a little better. He carried a big bucket filled with ice and sodas for the kids. From within the crushed ice, he took out a glass filled with tea topped off with a huge wedge of a lemon. It was his favorite drink. He handed the sodas to the kids while he sipped on his tea through a straw.

"So," asked Bess, " everyone get settled in?"

Steve looked over at Annie, who hadn't experienced all the events that the Zap-Gun Rangers had. She didn't know all of what went on, and it really should be a secret. But he was never good at keeping secrets from his daughter. Annie probably knew more than he thought, anyway. It was hard to hide what had happened in the town the month before.

"Yes," he said. "We got them into a few of the new houses on the south side." Steve and Portia Truly had been part of a group that built new housing around Three Winds for the growing town. It seemed like as good a place as any to let some of the refugees move in. "So many of them wanted to go see the country, or the rest of the world. They had only seen the land and sea, and heard our languages and TV shows. But they hadn't experienced everything."

Bess knew what her father meant. She had gone to a grocery store with some of the teenagers, who were shocked at all the different food they could buy, frozen, fresh, cooked, and especially the ice cream and treats they could try. It literally was a new world for them.

But a few were ready to be comfortable and safe. Exploring would come later. They just wanted a home, and Steve had worked with the agents to give them one. Working on a ranch or the nearby dairy farm was a big change, but a welcome one.

"So, Dad," asked Bess. "I'm guessing that the moon men were all rounded up out there in the mountains, right?" She had wanted to ask her father what he knew, but didn't want to pry.

"Yeah," Steve answered as he sat down beside her on a long chair. He took a sip of tea before going on. He looked a bit out of place in his jeans and boots, with his cowboy hat dipped low over his head. The only thing that fit in were are pair of fancy black sunglasses. Somehow, he made it all work.

"Lookin' good, Mr. T!" said Lydia, always the fashion consultant.

"You gotta get me some boss trunks like Jesse has," Steve yelled back. Jesse beamed with the compliment from the adult.

"Meanwhile, back at the ranch," said Bess in a sotto voce whisper to her father. She wanted to get him back on track.

"Back at the ranch, yes." He almost hoped Bess would be distracted. "So... well, Agents Phillips and Marsh sent in their boys," meaning a special group of Army soldiers, "along with a couple of those poor conscripts that the moon men had." They were young men forced to fight. "But, like I said, the fight was out of those fellahs. They realized that without any food or water, and no ship to get back to the moon, they better just give up and come peaceful-like. I'm betting they have joined their brothers from our earlier dust-up." He pointed back over his shoulder at the Crater far to the east.

"Dad," Bess began.

Steve saw the look in her eyes, and guessed what the question would be. It was time that a girl as curious as Bess would wonder this.

"Where did the moon men come from?" It was a fair question. "I mean, how did they get all that technology? They are human, right? They look just like us, they talk like us, well, they *can* talk like us," many of the people on the moon knew multiple languages from studying the Earth. "But how did they get there?"

Steve stuck his hand under his hat to scratch his head. This was a question he asked himself, and the others that had been involved in all the adventures up to this moment. He had even asked the people who had come from the moon.

"Honestly, kiddo," he took a serious tone, "they don't really know, so I don't *know*, either." This wasn't much help to her, but he had to be honest with his daughter. "They don't entirely understand the technology they have. They know how to use it, and they can repair it and power it, but they can't reproduce it. Neither can we, I think. I mean," he sighed contentedly, "let's face it, if your mother can't figure it out, then no one can."

"But how did they get it, then? And how did they get to the moon?"

"Okay, I know this is going to sound weird," Steve began. He reached into his pocket as he talked. "I got from them that they don't remember, even the old folks, ever being anywhere else except the moon, so they have been there for around 80-90 years, but like you said, they're human. I think they were brought there from here. From somewhere here, from Earth."

"Brought to the moon? By whom? No one had space ships back then. You're talking about around the Civil War. They barely knew about taking baths then. No one was flying to the moon. No one was flying except in a balloon!"

Steve remembered a quote he had heard, along with Bess, from the agents as they had met in his office long ago.

"No one on Earth," he said. He pulled out a small piece of metal from his pocket.

"I took this from the bus," he explained. "It was part of something like a history book, or a display. Take a look at this."

Steve handed the metal plate to Bess.

It was incredibly light for its size. It had a strange iridescent gleam to it, like it reflected an oily sheen, but it was smooth and cold to the touch. Bess accidentally squeezed it and the metal folded. "Oh, no," she said, "I'm sorry..."

But then the metal popped back, showing no signs of damage. "Yeah, I did the same thing," Steve responded. He crumpled it in her hand, and it sprung back open, still flat and smooth. "Look at the image."

On it there was some symbolic writing that communicated something. But within it was a strange shimmering image. It had depth, and moved as Bess shifted it in the light. It looked like a lenticular image, but with more depth. On the image was a tall strange figure, in a flowing cloak, with a long neck, hooded eyelids and a wide nose. It was only vaguely humanoid. "*What is that*?!"

Steve took the metal from her with a look that told her to hush. This was not something he wanted to share, even with her friends who had seen so much.

"I told you, I took this from their ship. I think it's a marker from long ago, when they were first brought to the moon."

"By that?" Bess asked, trying and failing to keep her voice quiet and calm. The radio only barely drowned out her rising exclamation. "Who is that?"

"I think that is who took them from the Earth and brought them to the moon."

"But who is that? Who are they?"

Steve looked around at the kids playing. He wondered how much of this perfect day would change if he said what he thought. But he had to tell someone.

No one on Earth.

That was the phrase he had heard. That was what he thought. The people on the moon were human. They were Earthlings.

"I know this is going to sound really wild..." he started.

"Go on..." Bess urged him.

"I think that these people," he pointed at the picture on the metal, "were from Mars."

Bess opened her mouth, but said nothing at first.

Then she whispered with her mouth dry...

"*Martians...*"

# About The Author

Joe Sledge is the author of the *Did You See That?* North Carolina travel series of books and his Haunting North Carolina ghost story collections. A native of North Carolina, his love of travel and exploration sent him across the county by car, airplane, or boat. On his first trip to the West Coast, Joe became fascinated with the deserts and plains along Route 66, along with the cultural history so prevalent to the area, which was so different than the coast of NC.

With a love of old time science fiction, an amateur study of Cold War era events, as guided by tales from his father, and a desire to write a book series that would appeal to his daughter and kids anywhere, Joe created Bess Truly, an adventurous teen with a fast horse and a quick draw.

Joe currently resides in North Carolina with his wife and daughter.